HEALING THE OMEGA

HOBSON HILLS OMEGAS: BOOK FOUR

C.W. GRAY

❀ Created with Vellum

AUTHOR NOTE

Thank you for returning to the Hobson Hills Omegas series! Here is a quick reminder of the names of Dean's sons: Yeo (married to Caden), Jackson, Jimmy, Jake, Jules, and Min.

CHAPTER 1

*D*ean Wagner slapped his alarm clock when it blared loudly. It silenced immediately, but he didn't get up. He was so tired after tossing and turning all night and knew it was a sign that today would be more difficult than usual. He groaned softly and sat up.

Beau snuffled in his sleep, starting to wake. The golden retriever slept sprawled across the empty side of the bed. He liked to cuddle at night and Dean appreciated it. He had never had someone or something to hold while he slept. Lucy, Dean's long-haired calico, slept at the end of the bed. She didn't even open her eyes, convinced it was too early to get out of bed.

He yawned and rubbed his eyes, looking around. The large master bedroom was completely dark, and he was tempted to lay back down. Damn, he was so tired. He definitely agreed with Lucy – staying in bed sounded wonderful. His leg told him that he had to get up and move around though. He threw the covers off, grumbling. Spring in Maine was a cold, wet, and muddy time, and he could feel it all in his bum leg.

After a hot shower, his leg felt a bit better, and he was fully awake. He headed to the nursery first. Min was almost a year old, and Dean knew he needed to start planning a birthday party soon.

"Hey, baby boy," Dean whispered.

Min was already sitting up and rubbing his eyes. He gripped his brown stuffed rabbit tightly and broke into a goofy little smile when he saw Dean.

"Papa," he said, holding his arms and rabbit up. Dean smiled as warmth filled him.

He picked Min up and changed his diaper quickly, then dressed him for the day in loose grey pants and a blue and grey shirt covered in bunnies. His son-in-law, Caden, loved rabbits.

"Your big brother Caden likes to cover you in bunnies, doesn't he?"

"Papa," Min said and gave Dean a wet kiss on his scarred cheek.

"Come on, little charmer," Dean said, picking Min up again.

He left the nursery and headed for Jacob's room next door. The cabin was the nicest home Dean had ever had, and he loved it. Once Caden had finished adding the huge master bedroom and renovating the attic, the house had five bedrooms and three bathrooms. Each of his boys had a bedroom of his own for the first time in his life.

He knocked on Jake's door, then cracked it open.

Jake was thirteen now and insisted on privacy. "Jakey," Dean said softly. "Are you up?"

"Mm-hmm," Jake mumbled from his bed.

Dean poked his head in and saw movement. Lola raised her head from where she slept at the foot of the bed. The beagle yawned and lay her head back down.

"You have thirty minutes to get dressed," Dean said. "Grab a shower first."

Jake pushed his covers back and yawned. His reddish-brown hair was a mess atop his head, and his blue eyes were sleepy. "Waffles?"

Dean smiled. "If you're ready in thirty minutes, you'll get waffles. If not, you can eat a banana and yogurt on the way to school."

He shut the door and went to Julian's room.

Jules was already up, reading a book his best friend, Harry, had lent him. Jules looked just like his older brother Jackson. His hair was brown, his eyes green, and freckles covered him head to toe. Two fat cats curled up with him, one on each side.

The grey and white tabby cat rubbed her head on Jules's knee while the white Persian stared at Dean, silently berating him for interrupting his Jules time.

"Grab a shower in my bathroom, sweetie, and get dressed. Waffles will be ready in thirty minutes," Dean said and stuck his tongue out at Pounce. The Persian just glared back.

"Yummy," Jules said, jumping up.

The tabby, Betty, meowed, startled by the movement, but made her way to Dean, weaving around his legs. Dean grabbed Jules as the boy sped out the door and kissed the top of his head.

"Eww, Papa," Jules said, then grinned. "Love you."

He ran toward Dean's room, and Dean made his way upstairs to Jimmy's attic room.

Jimmy was already up too, finishing something on his drawing board. Caden and his brother had fixed the attic up to be an artist's haven with plenty of windows and open space. Jimmy had covered the walls in framed copies of his favorite pieces, from renaissance artists to comic book covers.

"I can't believe you're already up," Dean said, peeking over Jimmy's shoulder. It looked like he was finishing a panel for a new comic book.

"Summer and I want to have the new comic out by the end of the week," Jimmy said, focused on his drawing.

James looked just like Dean and Yeo, his oldest brother. Their features showed off their Korean heritage, but the electric blue streaks in Jimmy's black hair were all him.

"Well, you have thirty minutes to get dressed and down to the kitchen if you want waffles for breakfast," Dean said. "Don't forget to shower."

"Okay," Jimmy said, distracted.

"Immy," Min said, reaching out a hand to grab his brother's hair. Jimmy looked away from his drawing and turned around, prying the baby's hand from his hair.

"Mini-boo," Jimmy said, grabbing the baby and

giving him kisses. "My sweet Mini-boo." He handed Min back to Dean. "I'll get ready now, Papa."

Dean tickled Min's belly and went back downstairs. "Good boy. That's the way to get them moving."

He headed to the kitchen, completely unsurprised that there was a large African-American man already working on breakfast. Waffles were Ray's specialty and his boys loved them. Dean loved them too.

"Hey," Dean said, yawning.

He set Min in his purple hippo baby walker, laughing when the little boy took off. He would definitely be walking soon. He turned back to Ray and watched the man move around the kitchen.

Ray plugged in the waffle maker and filled it up with batter. "Did you have nightmares again last night?"

"Yeah," Dean said. "I only woke up once, though, so I got plenty of sleep."

He didn't regret telling Ray about the dreams. Ray was his friend, and Dean trusted him. The beta never judged Dean or tried to make him act a certain way. He just listened patiently and offered comfort and a warm smile.

"Same thing?"

"Yeah," Dean repeated, sighing. "Same thing."

Almost every night, Dean had the same dream. He was back at the farm in Tennessee, and his dead husband, Simon, was still alive. Their last fight had been brutal. Simon had held him down and used a broken bottle to open up the scars on Dean's face.

5

Luckily, Jackson had taken the kids outside when the alpha had first started yelling.

"I know a great therapist, Dean. She could really help you deal with the trauma you lived through."

"I'll think about it," Dean said.

It's what he always said, and he really did think about it. He just always dismissed the idea. He didn't want to talk about Simon. He didn't even want to think about the asshole. When he had asked for help, not many people believed him. Simon was a respected pastor of a large and loyal church. Those that had believed Dean, simply didn't care what Simon did. He was the alpha, so they thought he could do what he wanted. Dean had gotten used to not talking about it.

He noticed a bright red coat hanging by the door where his old, ratty rain coat used to be. "What's that?"

"You needed a new raincoat, Dean," Ray said. "This one will keep you dry."

Dean picked it up and put it on over his sweater. "It fits perfectly!" He took it off and held it up, looking at the brand. "Outdoor Research? It wasn't expensive, was it?"

"No. Not at all," Ray said, voice going high.

He was lying. Dean always knew when the man fibbed. Not that he did it often or over anything important.

"You needed it, Dean, and I happened to find it. No big deal."

"You buy us too much," Dean said.

After almost a year of daily gifts, he had accepted that Ray was his guardian angel. His jobs and Caden's gift of the cabin allowed Dean to take care of his family. His eldest sons, Yeo and Jackson, had originally made a plan to fully support him, but Dean didn't want to be a burden. That didn't stop Ray and them from showering him and the boys with gifts.

"Jimmy needed those new pencils," Ray protested.

"Did Jules really need another hamster? Were two not enough?"

"He loves McCoy," Ray said. "Spock and Kirk needed a friend. They told me so."

"Hearing voices, are you?" Dean watched Min move his walker right behind Ray. "You have a Min behind you."

Ray looked over his shoulder and cooed. "Mini-boo. How's my baby boy?"

"Dada," he said, waving at Ray.

Ray's grin lit up the room. "Damn, but I love it when he calls me that."

"I'm sorry," Dean said, wincing. "He isn't old enough to understand, and I try all the time to get him to call you Ray."

It was even worse when they were all in public. More than once, a young man or woman had abruptly stopped flirting with Ray when they heard Min call him Dada. Every time, Ray just laughed and kissed the baby's chubby little cheeks.

"I like it," Ray said, shrugging. "Anyway, I'm making bacon and eggs too. It's cold out there and you'll need a warm meal in your belly."

"Thank you, Ray," Dean said, hugging the man

around his waist. He set his head against the beta's back. "You make every day so much easier."

Dean meant it too. Ray did a lot for them, but simply being there with his wide grin and cheerful personality made Dean's life so much better. He would make some lucky person a wonderful husband one day.

"It's time for my morning joke," Dean said.

"Did you hear about the sensitive burglar?"

Dean snickered. "No. What about him."

"He takes things personally," Ray said.

Dean could hear the grin in his voice and giggled against Ray's back. "I'm going to take care of the beasts, then I'll be back to eat. The boys should be down in about twenty minutes."

He forced himself to let Ray go and put his new coat back on. "It's so warm!"

"Good," Ray said, pleased. "Don't forget gloves."

"Yeah, yeah," Dean said, pulling his gloves on.

He smiled at Ray one more time and headed outdoors. It was still dark outside and nasty. Snow slowly melted, making it wet and cold.

Dean followed the gravel path to the big red barn, smiling like a loon. Damn, but he loved the outdoors, even when it was miserable. There was something about this place that soothed him. It was home.

He opened the door and Jules's miniature pig Petunia came running to him along with her brother Dandy and her sister Daisy. The three pigs had free reign of the barn and little nests in one of the stalls. Dean had installed a doggy door for them go outside when they wanted, but the spoiled brats preferred the warm barn. He couldn't really blame them.

"Hi, cuties," Dean said and took a minute to feed them. If they weren't eating, they'd be right under his feet.

"Moo!" A loud, impatient sound came from the back of the barn.

"Moo to you too, Miss Swiss," he said, grinning.

The Swiss dairy cow poked her head over her stall door. "Moo!"

"I'm coming," he said, opening her stall door. "Are you ready to be milked, girl?"

Miss Swiss's sister poked her head over the wall separating them. She was the quiet, sweet one. Her liquid dark eyes watched him intently.

"I'll be with you shortly, Brownie."

He milked the two cows and brought the milk to the little kitchen Gramps had insisted be added on when the barn was built. He poured the milk into glass bottles and set them in the sink. Then grabbed his frozen water bottles from the freezer. He set them around the bottles and ran cold water into the sink. His Swiss girls produced a lot of milk, but his boys went through it fast.

While the milk cooled, he fed and checked on the horses and donkey, then checked for eggs from the chicken coop. He let all the animals out into the pasture and put the cooled bottles of milk in the refrigerator, adding them to the sixteen bottles already there.

When he was done, he grabbed a dozen eggs and

two bottles of milk, then headed for the house, saying goodbye to the piggies when he went. He whistled as he limped along the path, pausing to appreciate the beautiful cabin. Warm light poured from the windows.

Beau, Lola, and the cats were lined up at their food bowls, munching on breakfast, by the time he got back. The boys were finishing their own breakfast, and he checked the time.

"Bus will be here in five minutes, guys. Jules, don't forget your science project."

"Oh, yeah," Jules said, stuffing the last bite of bacon in his mouth. He ran to the living room and came back with his lemon powered battery. "Almost forgot."

Ray handed him his lunch box, and Jules ran out the door with Jake and Jimmy, heading down the driveway.

"Jimmy really needs a car," Ray said. "He could drive the boys to school every morning then."

"He just got his license," Dean said.

It had taken his son longer than usual to pass his driving test. He... wasn't the best driver. Even John had given up on teaching him, and Dean's friend had been confident he could do it. Ray ended up stepping in and finishing the job.

"I don't know if I trust him to get them all there alive," Dean finally said.

"He's not that bad," Ray said with a laugh. "Plus, he won't get any better if he doesn't actually drive."

"I'll think about it," Dean said.

His job with Marco paid well and provided them with insurance, and his side jobs with Noah and Ernie gave him a chance to build up his savings. A car was a big expense, though, and Jimmy was saving all his money from his comics for college. He planned on majoring in art and specializing in drawing and illustration.

"Shawn bought a beat up Nissan a few weeks ago and has been working on fixing it up," Ray said. "It's not looking so bad now. Just saying."

He sat at the table with his own plate of breakfast and started eating. Dean piled a plate high with food and sat across from Ray. Dean stared at his plate, hiding his blush as he thought about Ray. Life was so damn good when Ray was here. He wished this was real. He wished Ray was his husband and the kids were his. He wished it never had to end.

"THANKS FOR HELPING, DEAN," Gramps said. The older man stretched his arms above his head. "Spring always means the fields need tilled and the earlier the better."

"Driving a tractor is a lot easier than chasing cattle around all day," Dean said with a laugh.

He had finished early with Marco today, and they had decided to pitch in with the rest of the Wilsons to get the gardens and fields plowed and ready to be planted.

"That's the truth," Marco said, jumping down from his own tractor. "If I have to pull another calf out of the mud, I'm going to scream."

"You love it," Dean said, smirking.

His boss just smiled and shrugged. The two men

worked well together. Marco didn't mind that Dean moved slowly. He often told Dean that he didn't mind his slow pace because Dean did the job well. Marco didn't suffer fools or lazy employees, so Dean knew he meant it.

"Marco," Grammy called. "Come help me with the drinks. We need to warm these folks up."

"Coming, Mama," he said, jogging to the truck where Grammy was unloading insulated cups of coffee.

"How's Ray doing today?" Gramps bumped his shoulder against Dean's as they walked slowly toward the truck. Dean's leg was starting to hurt, but it always did toward the end of the day.

"He's good. Watching Min and working from the house. He got to start a new investigation today, so he was all giddy," Dean said. The beta liked puzzles and had a mind like a steel trap.

"He's over at your house every day," Gramps said.

"He's a good friend," Dean said, smiling.

Ray really was his best friend. Well, Ray *and* Susan were his best friends. He could never forget the amazing woman who cared so much about him.

"I've seen the way he looks at you, Dean," Gramps said. "He wants to be more than a friend. Has for a long time."

Dean stopped walking, frozen, the vision of Ray and him together filling his head. He blinked a few times, then started laughing uncontrollably. Oh god, that was hilarious. Like Ray would want a forty-six-year-old man with more aches and pains than an eighty-year-old. Plus, did Gramps not see the people throwing themselves at Ray every time he went to town? Ray was gorgeous, sweet, and in high demand.

"Seriously, Gramps," Dean wheezed. "That's impossible."

It would be wonderful, but Dean didn't stand even a speck of a chance with Ray. Hoping for more would just hurt, and Dean had hurt enough in his life.

"Why would it be impossible?" Gramps huffed and stood with his arms crossed.

"To start, Ray is twelve years younger than me," Dean said, chuckling. "Plus, have you seen me?"

He waved to his face. A lot of the scars were faded, but they were still there. The emotional scars were far worse and what man would want to deal with them on top of the physical ones?

"Oh, I've seen you, Dean Wagner," Gramps said, cupping Dean's face in his hands. "You are a beautiful man, both inside and out."

Dean's eyes met Gramps's and he felt them water. The damn man saw straight into him.

"Well, now, what's going on here?" Grammy said, brow raised and hand on her hip. She winked as she handed Dean a cup of coffee.

"I'm telling this idiot how beautiful he is," Gramps said, shrugging.

"That he is," Grammy said, kissing her husband on the cheek. "Beautiful I mean, not an idiot."

She gave Dean a stern look. "You deserve happiness, Dean. I know you love it here, but there's an empty wanting in you and it breaks my heart. You are a beautiful soul and there are plenty here in Hobson Hills who see it. *You* just have to see it too."

"I don't know," Dean said quietly. "I do… I do feel it. The kids and our home make me happy, but I know there's something missing. I've just never gotten to want things of my own before."

"Think about what you want, Dean. Think long and hard on it," Grammy said. "When you're certain, I'm telling you now, it's yours for the taking."

CHAPTER 2

*R*ay e-mailed his report to his boss, Hort. After a day of chasing Min around the house and digging into the life of some banker in Wisconsin, Ray could use a diversion.

He gave Beau and Lola some loving, picked up Pounce and hugged him until he stopped hissing, then grabbed Min and checked on the critters in the barn.

Petunia was a people pig. She loved humans and came running as soon as the door opened. Her siblings were a little shyer, but Ray made sure to spend time with them too. He scratched their chins and bellies and gave them treats.

Then he went to visit his favorite. Dean's donkey was named Jackson, just like his son. Jules had gotten to name him when he was four, and since Jackson was his favorite thing at the time, he'd named the donkey after his brother. Jackson hadn't found it as funny as the rest of the family.

"Hey Jackie-boy," Ray said, scratching the donkey's

long ears. "Why are you in the barn today? There's a ray of sunshine outside, the first of the year, and you choose to stay in the barn."

The donkey brayed and settled his head on Ray's shoulder. Min giggled and patted the donkey with his hands.

Fuck, he wished this were real. He wished he was Dean's husband and the boys were his. He wished Dean was his man, a beta's omega. Omegas were meant for alphas though. Plus, Dean wasn't ready for all that, and he may never be ready. Of course, that didn't make Ray want it any less.

"Ready to start dinner, Mini-boo?"

Ray headed toward the house and saw the bus stop at end of the driveway. Jimmy, Jake, and Jules stepped off the bus along with some friends – Harry, Summer, Hannah, Tali, and Drew.

Ray was damn happy to see Drew. Bennett and Marco's newly adopted son was shyer than Daisy and Dandy. The young beta had come out to his former foster parents and been kicked to the curb. Now, he belonged to Bennett and Marco, but he was still having trouble believing it was permanent.

"Hey," Ray called, meeting them at the front of the house.

"Ray." Jules ran to him and hugged him. "I got an A on my science project. Ms. Beeler said it was really good."

"Good job, Jules," Ray said. "Your papa is going to be proud."

Jules nodded excitedly. "Since I got an A, can we have fried chicken for dinner? Please?"

"That's why he gets good grades," Jimmy said, ruffling Jules's hair. "He likes to pick out what we eat for dinner."

"You're not wrong," Jules said, grinning. He turned his big green eyes on Ray. "Please?"

"Okay, okay," Ray said with a laugh. "You all staying for dinner?"

A chorus of yeses answered him.

"Good deal. Boys, don't forget your chores."

"Come on, Drew," Jimmy said. "I'll show you how to milk a cow."

Ray arched a brow. That meant Drew would milk the cows instead of Jimmy. Ray shook his head. Jimmy was a good kid, but he didn't exactly love the farm. He did love his horses though.

"Harry! It's chicken time," Jules said, grabbing his friend's hand and running to the barn.

"He won't eat the chickens, will he?" Tali looked after Jules, worried.

"No," Ray said, grinning. "He just collects the eggs."

"Shew," Summer said, wiping her forehead.

Tali rolled her eyes and pushed her friend. "I knew he wouldn't really eat them."

"Sure you did," Summer said with a smirk.

"Summer can help me with the feeding," Jake said, huffing. "It will keep her out of trouble."

"Gee, thanks," Summer said but headed toward the barn.

"I want to visit with El Paso," Tali said, sniffing. Her

long earrings jangled as she jogged to catch up with the others. El Paso was Dean's horse. The huge guy looked fierce, but he was gentler than any animal Ray had ever met. He also adored Tali.

Hannah shook her head and pulled on Min's boot making the baby laugh. Marco and Bennett's daughter had grown a foot over the last few months, and boys and girls were definitely noticing the way she filled her clothes. It made Marco's eye twitch, which Ray found hilarious. The girl was completely devoted to her girlfriend, so Ray knew Marco had nothing to worry about.

"I'm here for the pigs, Mini-boo," she said. "It's all about the piggies."

She rubbed her hands together and cackled as she ran after her friends.

Ray waited until all the kids reached the barn, then shook his head. "We have a herd to feed today, Mini-boo."

He went into the kitchen and put Min in his baby walker. Min started rolling around the room, giggling when Lola and Beau chased him. Usually Jules helped him cook, but if Harry was anywhere nearby, Jules was with him.

Ray set out some light snacks for the kids, then started on dinner. About thirty minutes later, the backdoor slammed open and kids tromped in.

"Remove your shoes at the door," Ray said loudly. "Also, you remember your papa's rule. Homework before fun."

There was some grumbling, but they started

settling into groups in the living room. Jules and Harry cuddled close as they opened their backpacks to search for their homework.

Jimmy grabbed the snacks on the way through. "Thanks, Ray," he said, grinning.

He went to sit with Drew and the two started their homework. There were a couple of years between them, so Jimmy would end up tutoring Drew with his math before they were finished.

Ray hummed as he cooked, happy to be in Dean's home. Ray knew Dean and his family could manage without him. They had survived worse with the asshole alpha. He liked being there though. Dean had said Ray made things easier, and as long as Ray was alive, he would be there for him.

Even if Ray couldn't have Dean for his own. One day, Dean would find his alpha and Ray would have to step aside. Until then, he'd enjoy it while he could.

Right before dinner was ready, Dean came in the back door, removing his muddy boots and sopping wet raincoat in the mudroom. *Yeah, that was a good buy*, Ray thought.

"That smells so good, Ray," Dean said, moaning.

Ray swallowed. Damn, he did not need to hear that sound coming from Dean.

Dean leaned down and petted Beau. The dog wiggled around, tail wagging like crazy. Ray knew how he felt.

"Is it okay if I shower real quick?"

"Yeah," Ray said. "We'll wait on you. Oh, yeah. We

have a herd tonight, so we'll need to eat in the living room."

Dean smiled softly and picked up Min, kissing his face and tickling his belly. "I like it when we have a full house."

Ray liked it when Dean said *we*.

"I'll hurry," Dean said. He took Min with him and limped to his room. Ray would press him to take a bubble bath tonight after dinner. That usually helped ease the ache in Dean's leg.

"Ray?" A soft voice pulled his attention away from Dean. Drew stood at the counter.

"Hey," Ray said, trying to look harmless. The boy was almost shaking.

"Jimmy said you investigate things for the Wilsons and Bensons," Drew said.

"That's right." Ray smiled. "I work for a security company and do a lot of online investigations for them. On the side, I'm always available if a friend or family member needs me."

"Could... could you maybe look for someone for me?" Drew stuttered over the question. "Terry was a friend of mine at my last foster home. They stayed there for a year when they were twelve, then the jerks made Terry go, just like they did me."

"Yes," Ray said without hesitation. "I'll see what I can do. You call your friend *they*. Is there a reason for that? Also, what's your friend's full name? Do you know why the assholes sent them away?"

"They were an omega and the Smiths didn't like omegas," Drew said. "Then, they came out as gender fluid and my old foster parents about died. That's why I call them *they*. It was the pronoun they preferred. On top of all of that, Mrs. Smith found them kissing one of the other boys in the house. The Smiths could deal with Terry being an omega as long as they weren't a weird fag. That's the Smiths' words, not mine."

"That's so stupid," Ray said, shaking his head. "What is Terry's full name?"

"Terrence Wilmoth," Drew said. He bit his lip. "I thought, well, Papa and Dad don't mind me, and Nate is an omega and they love him a lot. Plus, they love Tali just the way she is, you know? So maybe they wouldn't mind if Terry was a gay omega and gender fluid."

"They wouldn't mind at all," Ray said, absolutely certain.

Those two men were meant to be parents to a horde of children. Ray finished cooking dinner and chatted with Drew. By the time Dean came back in, dressed in comfy clothes, dinner was ready. He poked his head into the living room.

"Come grab a plate and a drink, kids," he yelled.

They spread across the living room to eat dinner.

"Jules, are you sure you and Harry don't want to sit on the couch?" Dean fed Min a small bite of chicken and watched Jules and Harry cuddle in the dog bed.

"Nope. We like Beau's bed," Jules said, taking a huge bite of his chicken leg.

"If it's good enough for Beau," Harry said, shrugging. "It's good enough for us."

"Ray," Dean said, patting the seat beside him.

Somehow, it was the only spot left. Ray looked

around the room suspiciously, but none of the kids would meet his eyes. He sat next to Dean and they ate and talked.

"I'm going to borrow Gramps's tractor tomorrow and plow up a spot for a garden. I always loved having one and we missed out on it last year. It's a lot of work, but the fresh veggies are so good," Dean said, hiding his yawn. "Thank you for cooking dinner, Ray."

"Hey, I got to eat. You all got to eat. It works out," Ray said. If it kept him close to Dean and the kids too, so what?

"Was Min good for you today?"

"He's a good baby," Ray said, pulling Min's foot. The baby giggled, face covered with mashed carrots. "I'm just happy he doesn't try to use the litterbox like Linc did."

"Don't jinx us," Dean said, horrified. "He's about to learn to walk and next it's potty-training."

Ray cringed. It was coming. The terror was coming.

Dean poked him in the side. "It's time for my evening joke."

"What do cows most like to read?"

"Oh god, no. It's joke time," Jimmy said, burying his face in his hands. "Cover your ears, Drew. We don't want to chase you off."

Dean couldn't hold in his giggles, and Ray's eyes softened at the sound.

"What do cows most like to read?" Dean asked, trying to stifle his laughter.

"Cattle-logs."

$\sim$

RAY TRUDGED up the stairs to his apartment, reading Noah's texts. His friend was doing well with the horse therapy center, but he was still adjusting to life with no hearing. It had been about two years since he'd lost his hearing, and Ray knew he still had trouble. Noah just hated showing it. He was adept at reading lips and had gotten fairly good at sign language, but it was a daily struggle to stay connected to the people around him. Maybe that was why the man enjoyed texting so much.

N: Did you declare your love tonight?

R: Hardy har har, fucker.

N: Seriously, man. You need to at least ask him out before you waste away from pining.

R: He's not ready to date.

N: Nightmares?

R: Why did I tell you about that?

N: Because you were drunk and sad.

N: It was really awkward carrying you up the stairs to your apartment. By the way, your eighty-two-year-old neighbor thinks we're lovers. I told him that we were open to a third, but he said he was too old for that shit.

R: ANYWAY – yes, he still has nightmares.

N: You should let him decide what he's ready for, Raymondlicious.

R: I hate you. Go away.

N: Love you too, boo-boo!

Ray shut the door behind him and turned the locks. His apartment was neat and spacious. It was also completely silent, and he hated it. Elijah and Carter had tried to talk him into a cat, but he had resisted. Now, his pets were all at Dean's house. His life was at Dean's house. Fuck, he hated coming back here.

He sat on the couch and pulled his laptop out. He pulled up his file on Michael Cook, the fucker that raped Dean years ago. Ray couldn't do anything about Simon Wagner. That asshole was dead, killed by someone else he'd pissed off. He *could* do something about Michael Cook.

The man was a filthy rat and Ray had found a lot of dirt on him. He'd found a lot of people Cook had hurt. Ray just had to figure out what to do with it.

CHAPTER 3

*D*ean finished breakfast the next day feeling better than he had in a long time. The night before, he had taken a long, hot bath while Ray watched the kids, and he had slept peacefully for the first time in years.

"Thanks for breakfast, Ray," he said. "You're really okay with watching Min every day? I don't want to take advantage of you."

"We have this conversation every morning, Dean," Ray said, starting the dishes. "What's my answer?"

"You don't mind because you adore Min," Dean said, giving an exaggerated sigh. "Okay then. I'll see you tonight?"

"For sure," Ray said, giving him a look. "What do I say about dinner?"

"You love cooking for me and the kids, and I shouldn't take that away from you," Dean said, laughing. "I get it. I get it."

"Go enjoy all those animals you love," Ray said. "Min and I have stuff to do today."

Min looked up at him and waved his stuffed bunny. "Bye-bye."

"Bossy britches," Dean said. "The both of you."

He kissed Min's cheek and had to force himself not to kiss Ray too. He had *never* wanted to kiss someone so badly before. He darted out the door before Ray noticed his red cheeks. This was getting harder to handle every day.

Dean and Beau jumped in the beat-up truck Shawn had fixed up for Dean and drove by Farm Fresh, the Wilson family's store. He dropped off the extra milk and eggs he had from the week, then headed to Ernie's house.

Ernie Wilson was a school teacher in Hobson Hills, but he loved yarn and knitting with a passion. He had his own alpaca and sheep herds, but the morning feeding and check-in was hard for him to manage when he had to be at school at seven.

Dean took a drink of the coffee Ray sent with him and looked at Beau in the passenger seat. "Are you sure you want to be a work dog today? You have it good back at the house."

Beau just grinned at him.

"Okay, but don't give me those tired puppy eyes tonight."

Dean drove to both pastures, and they poured out feed and refreshed the hay. Then they topped off the water troughs. Ernie usually pampered his herds and gave them treats at night, so each animal was fat and happy.

Dean counted heads in each herd and petted and loved on the spoiled brats before leaving them for Noah's place.

Noah's horse therapy ranch was one of Dean's favorite places. It was expansive, with plenty of gentle riding trails, but the real joy were the horses. Noah had two large stables full of horses. The one Dean helped in was for the rescue horses he took in – the ones that needed to adjust to their new lives.

They needed lots of loving and care, and Dean adored them all. Some came in and just needed a quick check up before they were ready to go on rides and play in the pasture with the other horses. Then, there were some that needed a lot more care and time.

He parked and got out of the truck, Beau trotting beside him. The rescue stable was busier today than normal. The horses that were now healthy but still needed to get used to humans were at the front.

It was a little unusual, but Noah and two visitors were working through the nine horses, brushing and petting them and feeding them treats. Noah saw him and waved, then went back to his horse, showing the two men how to brush Stink Bug down. Normally, Noah would have them work with the gentled horses in the other stable.

Dean shrugged and headed toward the back. They had five horses that were still recovering from abuse and neglect. His favorite was Firefly. The dun gelding had come in extremely malnourished and with overgrown hooves. The farrier and veterinarian were both working with him, but it would take time.

"Hey, handsome," Dean said.

He got a handful of oats and fed them to the horse. He couldn't eat a lot at a time yet, but he was getting better every day. The horse nickered softly and settled his big head on Dean's shoulder.

"Are you my sweetheart?" He scratched the horse's ears and stroked his soft nose. "Come on, handsome." He led the skittish horse to a clean stall, then Dean washed down Firefly's stall and put fresh hay and water in it for him.

"Fuck. These horses are disgusting." One of Noah's new hires stepped out of the feed room. "Deaf boy should have just sold them to the slaughterhouse."

Dean bit his tongue and took a breath. Bruce was a jackass, but he was also big and an alpha.

"Hey, scar boy, I'm talking to you."

Dean rolled his eyes. Seriously? *Deaf boy* and *scar boy* were the best insults the idiot could come up with? They sounded like weird superhero names.

"Don't roll your eyes at me, omega!"

A hand clamped down on his arm and pulled him from Firefly's stall. Bruce shoved him against the stall door and pinned him there with his body.

The horses snorted and reared, banging against the stall walls.

Dean was suddenly back in Tennessee with Simon's body pressing his into a wall as he yelled and pressed the broken bottle to Dean's face.

"What the fuck?" Bruce's body was gone in seconds, and Dean shook as he slid down the stall door.

Beau's teeth clamped onto the back of the man's leg, and he dragged him away from Dean.

"Dean?" Noah crouched down next to him.

He looked at Beau. "Beau," he said and signed. "Stop."

Dean's dog let go of Bruce immediately and came to his side, whining. Dean buried his face against his fur. Firefly leaned his head down and mouthed Dean's hair, nickering softly.

"That damn dog bit me," Bruce yelled. "I want it put down. Now."

One of the visiting veterans knelt on Dean's other side and signed to Noah angrily. Noah's face turned red and he snarled. "Get the fuck out, Bruce. Now. You're fired."

"I want this fucker put down!" Bruce snarled and started forward again.

Beau growled low in his chest and Noah jumped up, standing in front of Dean.

"There are cameras everywhere, asshole," the visitor said. "I'm betting the dog was protecting his owner. Get the fuck out, or we can call the police and see what they say."

"Whatever," Bruce said, backing up. "This place is shit anyway."

He turned on his heel and headed toward the front. The other visitor watched him go with eagle eyes.

"Hey. Dean, isn't it?" The man at his side smiled

gently. "My name is Saul and my buddy over there is Emmet. Are you alright?"

"Yes, alpha," Dean said, then started crying. He hated that word – alpha.

"I'll get Susan," Noah said and signed. He pulled out his phone and texted Dean's best friend. His phone pinged and vibrated. "She's on her way." He sat beside Dean and leaned into him. "It's okay, Dean. It's okay."

Dean lost track of time, then Susan was there, kneeling beside him in her designer dress.

"Dean, what you're feeling isn't real and it'll stop soon. You are not back there with him. You're in Maine with me and Noah and Beau and these horses." She hugged him and grabbed his hand, pressing it to his chest. "Breathe in and out, sweetheart. Big breathes. In and out."

Dean took deep breathes, feeling his hand rise with each one.

"You are so strong, Dean. You survived him and you'll make it now. I swear," Susan said.

Dean focused on Susan's voice. He focused on Beau's warmth and Firefly's nickers. "I'm alright. I'm alright."

"Yes, you are, sweetheart," Susan said. She wrapped him in her arms and rocked him.

"I texted Marco," Noah said and signed. "He said to take today and relax. He also said he was hunting the fucker down, but I'm not supposed to tell you that."

"He need any help?" Saul grinned as he signed.

Noah rolled his eyes. "Come on, you two. Let's let Susan do her thing. We have horses to brush." He leaned down and hugged Dean. "I won't text Ray, but you need to tell him tonight."

"You want to get out of here, sweetheart?" Susan kissed the top of his head, then made a face. "You have horse drool in your hair."

Dean huffed out a laugh and reached up to pet Firefly's nose. "Good boy." He leaned into Beau. "You're a good boy too." His voice broke and he sobbed. "I'm such a weak idiot, Susan. All he did was press me against a wall. He didn't hit me or hurt me, but I'm a mess. I'm a fucking mess. I don't want to be a victim."

He leaned into her shoulder.

"Sweetheart, you aren't a victim. You're a survivor. What you went through was horrible." She stroked his hair. "I know you haven't dealt with it. You barely talk to me about it, and we talk about everything."

"I hate thinking about it," he said. "I dream about him every night. I don't want him in my days. He's dead. He's gone."

"Hey," Emmet said, squatting down in front of them. His expression was pained. "I swear I'm not trying to eavesdrop, but I get what you're going through."

Dean looked him up and down. "You're an alpha," he said. "How can you understand feeling powerless?"

Emmet gave him a sad smile. "Alpha, omega, beta – it doesn't matter. We can't control everything, especially not our own heads. What we can control is what we do about our problems. You have a past that you're struggling to deal with. I have memories that

31

haunt me, memories I want to forget. We can't run from it all, can we?"

"No," Dean whispered. He held Susan's hand, playing with her thin, elegant fingers. "No, we can't."

"We can do something about it," Emmet said. "I just started talking with a therapist. You could see one and start working through your memories."

"I know an excellent therapist that is just a few towns over. Also, I have the information for one that does video chat counseling," Susan said. She blushed when they stared at her. "I may have wanted to be prepared for this."

"I know I have a problem," Dean said. "When *he* died, I thought it would be all better, and it is better. The boys are safe and I'm so much happier." He looked at Emmet. "Thank you, Emmet." He settled his head on Susan's chest. "I'll go see the counselor, therapist, psychologist, whatever. Ray keeps suggesting it too."

"I'm glad to hear it," Emmet said. "If you ever want to talk, here's my number."

He pulled a card out of his pocket and Susan handed him a pen from her purse. He wrote his number on the back and handed it to Dean with a crooked grin. He joined Noah and his friend, leaving Dean with Susan.

"Thank you, sweetheart," Susan said. "I think it will help. You hold everyone in your family together, but you forget that you need care too."

"You and Ray take good care of me," Dean said. He wiped his eyes, then struggled to his feet. "I have some horses to take care of, then I'll go on home."

He scratched Beau's ears, and the dog went to sniff the feed room.

Susan stood and tried to dust off her dress, but there was no hope for it. She had hay in her hair and mud on her butt. She sighed, then shrugged.

"I'll keep you company." She tilted her head. "Somehow, when I'm with you, I always end up looking a mess."

"It's all the fun we have," Dean said. "Here, pet Firefly's nose. He needs loving."

"We all need loving, Firefly," Susan said and patted the horse.

CHAPTER 4

*R*ay put Min down for his nap and returned to the kitchen table and his laptop. He had a few things to look into today, but after that, he thought he might start a roast.

He sat and started working but looked out the window when he heard the familiar rumble of Dean's truck. He frowned and stood, watching from the window as Dean leaned his head back in the seat and closed his eyes.

Ray stood and headed for the door. By the time he reached Dean's truck, Susan parked her sleek Mercedes behind him.

"Dean, what's wrong?" Ray opened the door and helped Dean out of the truck. Beau hopped out behind him.

"Stupid stuff happened," Dean said, mumbling. His cheeks were pink with embarrassment.

"Dean," Susan said. "Your reaction isn't stupid, and neither are your feelings."

If Ray wasn't so worried about Dean, he'd laugh at the hay sticking out of Susan's hair. The woman was usually the walking, talking definition of a southern lady.

"Let's go inside and you can tell me what happened," Ray said.

He wrapped an arm around Dean, and the omega snuggled into his side, burying his face against Ray's chest. They walked slowly, Beau following behind. Ray helped Dean remove his boots and coat in the mudroom, then got him settled into his favorite recliner in the living room and covered his lap with a warm blanket. Lucy meowed and jumped up, settling on Dean's chest and purring.

"I'll make him a cup of tea," Susan said and went to the kitchen.

"Dean?" Ray knelt by his chair and cupped Dean's cheek. "What happened?"

"Noah's new hire got mad at me and pinned me to Firefly's stall door," Dean said. "That's all."

"That's all?" Ray repeated, incredulous. "Noah fired his ass, right?"

"Yeah," Dean said. "Beau pulled him off too, and Bruce said he wanted him put down." Dean's lip trembled.

"That shit isn't happening," Ray said. "He was defending you."

"That's what Saul said. He said there were cameras in the barn to prove it too," Dean said.

"Who's Saul?"

"A new visitor. Saul and Emmet are new and were

both there with Noah. It was so embarrassing, Ray. I just flashed back to Tennessee and my last fight with Simon."

Dean buried his face in his hands, and Ray wanted to find Bruce and beat the shit out of him. His hands shook and he grabbed Dean's wrists and gently tugged them down. Ray was a laid back man and feeling like this surprised him. It shouldn't, though, not really. It was Dean.

"Let me see those eyes, baby," Ray said.

Dean looked tortured. "I hate being like this. I just want to forget everything about Simon and Michael both."

"It's time you talk to a therapist, Dean," Ray said. "You can't run and hide from this."

"I know," he said and sighed. "You know a lady and Susan has some names too. I'll do it. I don't want to feel like this forever."

"Here we go," Susan said and set a tray with three hot cups of tea on the coffee table. She handed Dean a cup, then took one and sat.

"I texted Dr. Woodward, and she'll be happy to talk with you either in person or through video chat, whichever you're more comfortable with."

"That's the therapist I was telling you about," Ray said. "She's nice. David's daughter, Sadie, talks with her every other week. She's the one who told me to suggest her to you."

"Does everyone know I'm crazy?"

"You aren't crazy," Susan said. "I hate that word." She shook her head. "You've been through some horrible things and need a neutral person to talk to about it. There's absolutely no shame in that."

"She's right, baby," Ray said, rubbing a big hand through Dean's hair. "Sadie sees her and you don't think she should be ashamed, do you?"

"No," Dean said. "Of course not." He sighed. "Okay. When does she want to talk? I think I'd prefer video chat if one of you will show me how to use it."

Susan jumped up and checked her phone. "She's can talk with you right now, if you'd like."

"I'll get my laptop set up for you, alright?" Ray waited until Dean nodded.

He ran to the kitchen with Susan and they set up a login and password on Dr. Woodward's site, then got the call ready.

"Dean, it's ready," Susan said.

Dean held Lucy in his arms and sat at the table. Dr. Woodward's smiling face greeted him.

"I just talk and she hears me?"

"That's right, Dean," Dr. Woodward said kindly. "It's nice to meet you."

Susan and Ray backed out of the kitchen and left him to talk with the therapist. Ray fell into his chair and leaned his head back.

"That fucker didn't hurt him, right?" Ray asked.

"No," Susan said. "He scared him quite a bit, and I think he would have done worse if Beau hadn't been there."

Ray growled and Susan glared at him. "Don't you dare get growly, Ray. Dean needs you right now and your anger won't do you any good."

"I know," Ray said, running a hand over his face. "I'm not really a violent person, but it kills me that someone could be cruel to Dean."

"I know, sweetie, but you are so important to him," she said. "Your steadiness and good nature are what he needs, not some macho-alpha bullshit."

Ray looked at her in surprise. "You said bullshit."

She nodded smartly. "It was called for."

Ray grinned for a second before the rest of her words settled in. His heart grew heavy. "He's an omega. They're meant to be with alphas. They're meant to be protected."

Susan blinked for a moment, then groaned. "You actually believe that, don't you? Is that why you haven't started a romantic relationship with him?"

Ray shrugged and looked away. "There are a lot of reasons Dean and I aren't meant to be."

"Well, this reason is stupid," Susan said. "Biologically, alphas and omegas are more likely to produce children, but it's like saying only men and women should be together. Are you saying Carter and Elijah shouldn't be together? What about Yeo and Caden?"

"No," Ray said. "They're meant to be. You can tell it just by looking at them." He petted Beau's ears when the dog put his head in Ray's lap. "They're alphas and omegas though. My dad always told me betas stick with betas."

"Your dad is an idiot," Susan said. "We don't get to choose who we fall in love with, Ray."

"Yes, we do," he said, frowning. "Carter and Caden

chose well is all. What about you and John. Are you telling me you didn't choose John?"

Susan smiled wide. "I *didn't* choose him. I definitely didn't want to love John when we first met. He wasn't the first person I loved, you know."

"What?" Ray sat up straight.

"During my freshman year of college, I met a young man, Josiah. He was an art student and an omega. We got to know one another and we both fell hard," Susan said, smiling sadly. "My parents were furious, but I didn't care."

"What happened?"

"He got sick," she said. Tears filled her eyes. "Cancer." She wiped her eyes. "He went through treatment after treatment, but it wasn't enough."

"Susan," Ray said gently. "I'm so sorry."

"You can't tell me that the love I felt for him was wrong, Ray. I'm not an alpha, but I loved Josie with everything in me."

"You're right," Ray said, sighing. "I know my dad is wrong about a lot of things. It's just been so ingrained in me, you know?"

"Then uproot it," Susan said sharply. "There's something special in the way you look at Dean, and I know he wants you too."

"How did you meet John?" Ray leaned back.

He would think on it. He knew Susan was right, but it was hard to fight his dad's voice. Dean was worth fighting for though. He thought about Tali and Thacher and felt like a coward for hiding his feelings.

"A couple of years after Josie died, I graduated

college and went back home. My parents set me up on dates with all the eligible men they knew," Susan said and rolled her eyes. "I didn't fight it. I didn't think I'd ever love again so I didn't care anymore."

"How did it go?"

"It was horrible. They were all wealthy, selfish bastards." She smiled softly. "Then, there was one date that wasn't awful. I tried my best to dislike him, but the man was just too special. I hate that I met John through my parents, but he was worth swallowing my pride."

"Do you love him as much as you did Josie?" He shook his head. "Shit, Susan. I'm sorry. That's really personal."

"I do," she said without any hesitation. "I still love Josie, and I always will. They are so different from each other, but I love them equally." She leveled a stare at Ray. "John is an alpha, you know, and I am not an omega."

Ray grinned. "I get your point, Susan. A beta and an omega would be alright together."

"You and Dean would be alright together," she corrected. "We are far more than just a gender or a classification, Ray."

"You're right," he said thoughtfully.

What if Jimmy, Jake, or Jules fell in love with another omega or a beta? Ray would want them to be happy and wouldn't care. Why should it be different for himself?

Dean came into the living room, putting an end to the conversation. He looked drained.

"Well?" Susan sat forward, eyes worried.

"That was... tough," Dean said. "It was good too. We're going to set up a weekly session."

"Oh, Dean," Susan said and jumped up to hug him. "I'm glad you're taking this step."

"Me too," Dean said. He looked at Ray, eyes questioning. "I closed the screen when our talk ended and I saw a file on your laptop, Ray."

"Shit," Ray said, wincing.

"Why are you investigating Michael Cook?" Dean asked.

Susan's eyes widened, and she turned to look at him too.

"He hurt you," Ray said simply. "He's not a good man and he fucking hurt you."

"It was a large file, Ray," Dean said. "Have you been working on it since we met?"

"Yeah," Ray said, shrugging. "I'm not sure what to do with it all yet."

"Why would you do all of that? The time it had to have taken." Dean shook his head, amazed.

"It's my way of protecting you," Ray said. "He hurt you and I can't undo that. I can do this though."

"But why? It had to have taken months, Ray," Dean said, pressing.

"I would do this for any of my friends, Dean," Ray said honestly. He took a breath and looked at Susan before turning back to Dean. "For you, though, it's different. I feel more for you than I should and this is the only way I can show it."

"What do you mean?" Dean's voice was quiet and uncertain.

"You aren't ready for anything romantic," Ray said. "You may never want a relationship, but I care for you." He shrugged again. "I don't have any expectations, Dean."

Fuck, fuck, fuck. Did he really just tell Dean he loved him?

Dean looked at him, shocked. "No expectations?" His face grew angry. "No *expectations?*" He yelled the last word and stood, stalking to his room and slamming the door.

Beau and Susan looked at him, surprised looks on both their faces. Beau whined.

"What just happened?" Ray stared at Dean's closed door.

He had imagined telling Dean about his feelings a lot of times, but he'd never pictured him getting angry about it.

"Hmm," Susan said, thinking. She tapped her chin. "I think I know what happened." She arched a brow and glared at him. "If I'm right, Ray, then you had best get ready to grovel."

She stood and went to Dean's door, easing it open and sticking her head in. After a moment, she disappeared inside.

"What did I do wrong, Beau?"

The dog just watched him steadily, brown eyes judging him. He sighed and headed to the nursery, Beau following behind.

"I'll check on Min and start dinner, Beau. Then, I'm making chicken potpie. It's Dean's favorite and I guess I'm groveling."

CHAPTER 5

*D*ean washed his face then patted it dry with a hand towel. He was so tired of crying.

Ray cared for him. The handsome, wonderful man wanted to be with Dean. He should have been elated, but the idea that Ray didn't expect Dean to ever be ready for a romantic relationship hurt so damn much. It once again pointed out that he was a victim and maybe he always would be.

"Dean?" Susan's voice came from his bedroom. "I'm coming in, alright?"

He didn't say anything, and seconds later, she stood beside him, staring at him in the mirror.

"Ray is a great guy, but he isn't perfect, sweetheart," she said.

"I'm just a victim to him," Dean said harshly. "Someone who needs to be treated carefully and taken care of."

"I don't think that's true," Susan said. "The heat in

his eyes when he looks at you isn't from sympathy or pity."

"Then why didn't he say anything? Why did he wait so long to show interest?"

"There are a lot of reasons, sweetheart. Honestly, I think that maybe he is trying to protect his own heart," she said.

"From me?" If Dean held Ray's heart, he would treasure it.

"You." Susan turned around and hopped up, sitting on the edge of the vanity. "I think he worries that if you aren't ready for a relationship and he pushes for one, he'll lose your friendship. Then his heart would be broken."

"I can understand that. I worry too, but who the hell gets to decide when I'm ready for a relationship, Susan? Who?"

"You do," she said softly. "Dean, this morning you finally admitted that you need to deal with the trauma of your past. Like it or not, you *are* still recovering, both mentally and emotionally, from what that alpha put you through. Is it really so hard to accept that Ray didn't want to add to your burden?"

"I want Ray to see me as I am now. The man I've become isn't the same one that sat back and took Simon's abuse," Dean said. "I didn't know I could take care of my family on my own. I didn't know there were options for omegas. I didn't even realize I could stand up to Simon. Not until I did it."

Susan looked startled. "Dean, we all see the man you are. No one thinks of you as weak. The fact that you were able to protect your children for so long shows us all exactly how strong you are. That man never once laid a hand on your boys. Why is that?"

"I wouldn't let him," Dean said, voice barely above a whisper. "I was good at distracting him." He sighed. "What do I do to convince Ray I'm ready for a relationship?"

Susan smiled slowly. "Today is a day for new beginnings, Dean."

"Yeah." He nodded.

He'd taken the first steps by talking with Dr. Woodward. She wanted to see him again and had warned him moving forward wouldn't be easy. He was ready to do it. He thought of what Grammy had said the other day. She said he needed to decide what he wanted. He knew what he wanted.

"I want him to have expectations, Susan. I want him to expect me to care for him too. I want him so damn much, but I don't want him to look at me and see the omega Michael Cook raped or the omega whose alpha father forced him to marry a cruel asshole. I want him to see me. Dean. What do I need to do?"

Susan looked thoughtful. "Have you ever given him any indication that you want to be with him?"

"I dance with him," Dean said, blushing.

"You dance with me too," she said.

"Not like I dance with him," Dean said and shook his head. "Sometimes at night, when my leg doesn't hurt too much, we dance real close in the kitchen while the kids finish their homework."

"Why haven't you told me about that? Oh, never mind," she said, smiling. "Anything else?"

"I tell him how much I appreciate his help every day," Dean said.

"Oh, that isn't good."

"What?" Dean frowned. Why would appreciating Ray be bad?

"Maybe he thinks you see him as the *safe guy*," Susan said.

"Huh?"

"It means that he thinks you only see him as a close friend. Someone to hug and cuddle with, not kiss."

"I want to kiss him," Dean said, gasping. "Very much."

"Then, we need to let him know that," Susan said, smiling.

"I don't like games," Dean said, suddenly tired. "Dealing with Simon was exhausting, and I don't want to play at this."

"No," Susan said, shaking her head. "No playing. Be clear and honest."

"Okay." Dean took a deep breath and let it out. "I'll be right back."

He turned and went in search of Ray. He found the beta in the kitchen, talking to Min and Beau.

"The secret to a good crust, Mini-boo, is to sift the flour first," Ray said.

Min stared up at Ray from his baby walker. He chewed his fist and watched Ray's movements carefully. Beau watched them from his favorite spot under the table.

"Ray?" Dean almost laughed when Ray spun around and flour went everywhere.

"Fuck. Dean? Are you alright? Do you need something?"

"I'm forty-six years old," Dean said.

"I know," Ray said. "Your birthday is in September."

"I can't have any more children."

"You have six sons and two grandbabies, three counting Summer. I think you'll be okay," Ray said, smiling.

"I have nightmares almost every night, and there are times I panic and flashback," Dean said.

"That's completely understandable," Ray said, slowly. "That's why you're talking to Dr. Woodward."

"I have scars, Ray," Dean said, gesturing to his face. "They're faded, but they'll always be there."

"Dean. I think you're the most beautiful man I've ever seen. Those scars are just part of what shaped you into the person you are today."

Ray's eyes were soft and made something shift in Dean's chest. Dean pressed a hand to his heart, feeling its beat.

"Would you go on a date with me Sunday afternoon, around two," Dean asked.

Dean held his breath. Sundays were when the kids went to visit with Jackson and Yeo in town. Usually Dean went too, but it was one of the few times he didn't have the kids, so it was also the best time for a date.

"A date?" Ray stared at him, dumbfounded.

Maybe Susan was wrong about this. Maybe the

reason Ray hadn't made a move was because he didn't want to be more than just friends.

"You said you cared about me," Dean said softly. "As more than just a friend."

"Yes," Ray said, nodding. He blinked several times. "I want to be with you more than anything."

"Then, how about that date? That's what people who are interested in each other do, right?" Dean held his breath.

"Yes," Ray said, voice stronger this time. "Yes. A date sounds wonderful."

"Good," Dean said, relieved.

He turned to leave but looked over his shoulder. He narrowed his eyes. "Oh, and Ray, I am the only one who decides what I'm not capable of. Alright?"

Ray grinned. "Yeah. I see that now."

Dean gave Ray a stern look. "Are you making me chicken potpie?"

"Yes, sir." Ray's grin grew wider.

"Then I forgive you. Just this once." Dean nodded and left, going straight to Susan.

She was trying to clean the hay out of her hair.

"I did it," he said. "We're going on a date Sunday."

She squealed and spun him around.

"Finally," she said and hugged him.

"I've never been on a date. How sad is that?" Dean yawned. "I think I'm going to shower and take a nap. Today has been exhausting." He hugged Susan tightly. "Thank you so much for being there for me."

"There is nowhere else I would rather be. I'll let you rest, sweetheart. John is waiting at home. He's already putting together a defense just in case that horrible man tries something. He is also calculating bail money in case Marco murders the man." She kissed his cheek and headed to the door. "I'm coming over Saturday. We need to plan your date."

She shut the door behind her and he smiled. A date.

Dean yawned again and quickly showered the morning off his skin, then dressed in his most comfortable pajamas. He crawled into bed and burrowed under the covers. Beau hopped up and took his normal spot, and Lucy crawled over Beau and curled up on Dean's pillow, next to his head. He smiled softly as he fell asleep. He had a date with Ray.

He slept soundly until someone pounced on him. A familiar body wiggled between Dean and Beau and threw a thin arm over him, hugging him.

"Papa, are you awake?"

He opened his eyes and smiled at Jules. "I am now. Are you back from school already?"

"Yep. We've been home for a while. Why are you sleeping? Ray said to leave you alone, but I was worried."

"I had a bad day and needed a nap," Dean said.

He didn't lie. His boys had witnessed enough of the fighting between Dean and Simon that sugarcoating anything didn't work anymore.

"Was it a bad day like before?" Jules's lip trembled. "Ray won't let anyone hurt you, and we can go to the hospital now."

Dean's already fragmented heart broke a little more. He hated everything his boys had been through. If he

49

C.W. GRAY

had known he wouldn't have lost custody of them, he would have left Simon years ago.

"No," Dean said firmly. "Those days are long gone, baby boy. Today was just a little more stressful than usual, and I needed extra sleep."

"Like Mini-boo does?"

"Just like Min," Dean said and hugged his son.

"Ray made chicken potpie. It's your favorite," Jules said. "Gramps fixed up the ground for our garden, and Jimmy got to drive the tractor."

Dean smiled. With the emotional rollercoaster that morning, he had forgotten about wanting to get that done today.

"That was nice of them," Dean said.

"We did all our chores too. Petunia says hi."

"I'll have to give her extra scratches in the morning," Dean said. "How was school?"

"It was okay," Jules said, shrugging. "Nothing exciting but nothing boring either."

"Sounds like school." Dean smoothed the hair back from Jules's forehead. "Did you get to see Harry today?" Jules's best friend was a year younger than him, so they usually only got to see each other outside of school.

"Only before class started," Jules said with a pout.

He nibbled his lip, thinking hard. Dean waited and let his son process his thoughts. Jules was a thinker.

"Ray isn't like *him*, Papa. You know that, right? We really like him."

"Ray isn't at all like your alpha father," Dean agreed. "He's a good man and I like him too."

"We all sneak and watch when you dance together

50

in the kitchen," Jules confessed. "He makes you smile and laugh." Jules ran his hands over Dean's face. "I love it when you smile and laugh, Papa. We all do."

"Ray makes us happy, doesn't he?" Dean asked.

He knew that Ray meant a lot to the boys and it made things more complicated. The thought of them all together, as a family, made it worth the risk.

"We talked about it," Jules said. "Jackson, Jimmy, Jake, and me."

"About what?"

"You and Ray," Jules said. "Jimmy said Ray likes you a lot and probably wants to kiss you. We decided that we're okay with it as long as he doesn't make you cry."

Dean smiled. "Really?"

"Ray makes you shine brighter," Jules said, nodding. "He likes us too."

"We're going on a date Sunday," Dean said.

"What's today?" Jules asked and scrunched his face up, trying to think.

"Thursday, March 10th," Dean said. "Why?"

"Jimmy wins then," Jules said, giggling. "Jackson and Jimmy made a bet about when you and Ray would finally go on a date."

"You boys are terrible," Dean said, snorting. "How did you even know Ray and I wanted to date?"

It seemed like everyone but the two of them knew what was going on.

"I told you," Jules said. "Jimmy said Ray wants to kiss you, and Jimmy knows these things, Papa."

Dean rolled his eyes. Maybe he needed to have a talk with Jimmy about what kinds of things he knew.

CHAPTER 6

"There is no way Elijah isn't going to notice her, Carter," Ray said, shaking his head.

He stood with Carter, Ernie, Juan, and Noah. The men signed their conversation as they spoke for Noah's benefit. Together, they watched the black sheep walk to the pile of hay. Carter and Elijah's other animals stood around the pile, munching on a late breakfast. The sheep's little tail flicked back and forth as she stood between Pooka, a jersey cow, and Banjo, a miniature donkey.

"Look at that. Snuggles blends right in," Carter said. His dog Hotdog sat at his feet, panting. "She doesn't take up much space and everyone else here is bigger than her. It could be months before Elijah notices."

"You keep telling yourself that," Juan leaned against the fence with a grin. "How did Doc talk you into this one? Wait. Why were you even at the clinic? I fixed the broken pipe yesterday."

Carter shrugged, eyes guilty. He pet Hotdog's ears.

"I may stop and visit him sometimes. The man's family all live out-of-state now. He gets lonely."

"Lonely?" Juan laughed uncontrollably, and Ray couldn't help but join in.

"What?" Carter looked confused.

Ernie patted Carter's back. "Mrs. Sutherland and Mrs. Odell don't let him get too lonely. It's not common knowledge, but they're a throuple."

"Seriously?" Carter's eyes widened comically and his mouth fell open. "That bastard played me again. I stop by and visit with him at least once a week." He looked at Ray. "By the way, do you think Jules wants a guinea pig?"

"Where did you get that sheep?"

Elijah popped up next to the four men, and they all jumped. Billy, Elijah's goat, left the hay pile and wandered over, bleating a hello. Elijah scratched his head.

"Carter! I'm talking to you," Elijah said sternly.

"What sheep? I don't see any sheep," Carter said, eyes avoiding his husband.

Elijah just stared at Carter, their son Connor perched on his hip.

"Okay, okay. Dr. Grover couldn't find Snuggles a home, so I agreed to take her in. Look, she gets along with everyone." He waved toward the pasture.

"Where's Coop?" Ernie asked.

"He wanted his nails painted like Olive's, so Zoe and Olive are giving him a manicure and pedicure at the house." The omega shook his head and sighed. "Oh, alpha-mine. What am I going to do with you?"

Carter's eyes brightened and Ray winced, moving fast and covering Carter's mouth with his hand. "I'm not sure we really need to hear what he wants you to do with him."

"Why, hello there, Raymondlicious," Elijah said, eyes dancing with mischief. "Do you know what Susan told Caden who told Zoe who told me?"

"Huh?" Juan cocked his head.

"Ray has a date tomorrow," Elijah said, smiling wide.

"Really? Who with?" Carter asked. "Why didn't you say anything? You haven't dated anyone since you moved here."

"Is it that new waitress at the diner? She eye-fucks you every time we go there," Juan said.

Elijah, Ernie, and Noah shared looks.

"How can you two be so oblivious?" Noah asked. "Who has Ray been pining after for almost a year?"

"Well, it can't be the waitress," Juan said, frowning. "She's just been in town a couple of months."

"David?" Carter guessed, face doubtful. "He's married though."

"You two are ridiculous," Elijah said. "What do you even talk about at your poker games?"

"It's Dean," Ernie told them all, smiling at Ray.

"Yeo's dad?" Carter looked surprised. "I thought you two were just friends."

"Yeah," Juan said. "I mean, you go to his house every day and spend a lot of time with his family... Wait. Oh, I see it now."

"Anyway," Elijah said, making a face at Ray's friends. "Where are you two going?"

The omega wiggled in place, excited.

"I don't know," Ray said. "Dean didn't say."

Elijah gasped. "How can we get excited and plan ahead if we don't know where you're going?"

Ray grinned, then grabbed his phone when it rang. He looked at the screen. "Excuse me, guys."

He walked toward the barn and answered his phone. "Hort. What can I do for you?"

"Ray," Hort said, voice grim. "You know your little side project?"

"Michael Cook," Ray said slowly. "Yeah?"

"A couple of months ago, I put some feelers out for information on him. I have connections that you don't, so I thought it might help," Hort said.

"Oh, thanks," Ray said, surprised.

Hort hadn't mentioned Cook since their first conversation, so he had honestly thought his boss had forgotten about Ray's private investigation.

"One of my contacts gave me some information about his business that's a little worrying."

"His business? That's the one area he's been legit," Ray said.

"It was when his son Yeo was in charge of it," Hort agreed. "The new CEO is the problem. From what I can tell, Michael and his father had a hard time finding someone to step into Yeo's shoes. In the process, they alienated a lot of their customer base which caused profits to drop."

"I noticed that trend," Ray said. "Can't say it breaks my heart."

Hort laughed. "Yeah. I get that." He cleared his throat and continued. "The board started putting pressure on Michael, and Yeo wasn't coming back. Richard is too old to effectively lead the company, and Michael is more interested in spending the profit than in taking care of Cook Enterprises."

"That's where my information led me," Ray said. "What have you found out?"

"Michael turned to an old university buddy for help – Davis Vandenburg," Hort said.

"Oh, that stupid fuck," Ray said. "How bad is it?"

Vandenburg was a big name in drug trafficking. Publically, he was a wealthy, southern gentleman from a prominent family, but the FBI had multiple investigations going on the guy.

"Bad," Hort said. "Cook put one of Vandenburg's guys in place as CEO. The FBI are watching them closely. They're certain Vandenburg is using Cook Enterprises to import drugs."

"Could this spill over to his family?" Ray worried about Cook's kids.

Yeo and Summer were fully separated from the family, but Lowell and Derek still lived in Nashville. Fuck, Lowell was only seventeen. Fawn couldn't be counted on for help either. Derek, Lowell, and Summer's mother was a vapid socialite, and there was no getting around it.

Fawn and her sons had visited Yeo last summer, and the woman had spent the whole time at the bed and breakfast or shopping in town. She and Summer had managed to dodge one another for the entire two weeks. Ray didn't understand how she could so easily toss her daughter aside.

"Yeo and Summer should be fine from Vandenburg, but the others could be at risk," Hort said, echoing Ray's own conclusions. "My contact told me all of this for a reason though."

"So we could help Fawn, Derek, and Lowell?"

"No," Hort said. "The FBI are doing their best to make sure they stay safe. Their investigation isn't exactly a secret, but Vandenburg doesn't seem worried. The agents have already spoken to Fawn in secret. She took Lowell and Derek to France on vacation."

"What's the problem then?"

"Michael is pissed at Yeo," Hort said.

"I gathered they weren't too happy with him," Ray said dryly. Last year, Richard Cook had tried to force his grandson back into the CEO position by suing for custody of Summer and Linc.

"Yeah, well, now Michael has some shady-ass resources," Hort said. "While Yeo and Summer are likely safe from Vandenburg, we're worried Michael may try to retaliate against Yeo. Two of Cook's personal rivals have already disappeared."

"Fuck," Ray said, rubbing his hand across his face. "What can we do?"

"Keep someone with him," Hort said. "It will be at least a month before the FBI closes in. I'm sending two of my guys up there to help out, but it'll be a day before they get there."

"Hort," Ray said, surprised. "Thank you."

"You're a good guy, Ray, and I know you love your friends like family," Hort said. "We take care of our own."

"Okay," Ray said. "I'll talk to everyone today, and we'll keep someone on Yeo."

The call ended and Ray watched his friends laugh at Carter as he begged Elijah to let him keep Snuggles. This really sucked.

"Ernie has a herd of sheep, Carter," Elijah said. "Why can't he take her?"

"Snuggles is a black sheep," Carter said. "Her wool won't dye like the others."

"So? He doesn't have to use her wool for yarn if he doesn't want to." Elijah bounced Connor on his hip.

"She belongs with us, baby. I love her." Carter's face looked pitiful.

Noah caught sight of Ray's grim expression and his smile turned to a frown. "What's wrong?"

Ray walked back slowly. "Yeo's alpha father has got mixed up in some dangerous things. I can't be too specific with the details, but Hort is afraid that Cook will send someone to hurt Yeo in retaliation for leaving Cook Enterprises."

"Shit," Carter said. "We need to keep an eye on him."

"Hort is sending two guys up to help with that," Ray said. "It'll take a month for Cook to be dealt with, so we need to have someone with Yeo at all times."

"The three of us can work with Hort's guys," Juan said.

Noah smacked him, glaring.

58

"Oops. I meant the four of us," Juan said. "Sorry, little alpha-man. Sometimes I forget you have military training."

Ernie cleared his throat. "I may be an omega and a school teacher, but I can still help keep watch for bad guys."

"Okay. Okay. The five of us," Juan said, throwing his hands in the air.

Carter eyed Ray. "Are you alright with that?" Carter knew about Ray's aversion to fighting. Ray was a live and let live kind of guy.

"Damn right I am. It's Yeo," Ray said. Dean would be crushed if something ever happened to his son. Everyone would be. He shook his head. "I need to go talk to Yeo and Dean. I'll stay with Yeo tonight. Juan, can you spot me in the morning?"

"Sure thing," Juan answered. "We'll set up a rotation."

Ray nodded and turned to leave. Carter and Hotdog followed him.

"The timing sucks here, but how about that guinea pig," Carter said. "It would make a very romantic gift for your date."

"You already have it, don't you?" Ray eyed his friend, trying not to laugh.

"She's in the barn. I have a cage and food ready for her," Carter said.

～

"She's beautiful," Dean said, petting the brown, black,

and white guinea pig. "She's so big. I didn't know guinea pigs got this big."

Ray smiled softly as he watched Dean hug his new pet. The boys struggled not to laugh as their papa pampered the guinea pig.

"I'm going to name you Bonny because you're so darn pretty. We'll get you a ball like each of the hamsters have, and you can roll around with me all day," Dean said.

Jules tugged on Ray's arm. He whispered in Ray's ear. "I know you brought her for me, but Papa is in love. It's okay though. I have Spock, Kirk, and McCoy."

Ray hugged the boy to his side and ruffled his hair. "Thanks," he said. Min's walker rushed by, rumbling loudly as the boy scuttled around the living room.

"Papa, I think Yeo and Jackson are here," Jake said, looking out the window. "I thought we were seeing them tomorrow so you and Ray could go make out in private."

Ray snorted and Dean rolled his eyes. The boys were a little too accepting of Ray's interest in their papa.

"Ray needs to talk to them," Dean said. He gave Ray a trusting look and nodded.

Ray's heart thumped. Dean hadn't seemed a bit worried when Ray told him about the trouble coming their way from Cook. He simply said he knew Ray and the others would keep Yeo safe.

"You boys are going fishing with Uncle John while I work on planting the garden," Dean said.

"Won't you need our help?" Jimmy watched his papa worriedly.

Ray saw John pull up outside. Good timing.

"Bah," Dean said, waving his hands. "Susan and I can handle it. You know how much I enjoy it."

Ray nodded in agreement. He really did love working outside.

"I'll catch a fish for you, Papa," Jules said, running out the front door.

"I'll catch more," Jake said, following his brother.

Jimmy grabbed their backpack of snacks before leaving. "Uncle John, can I drive?"

"Hell no," John said, voice horrified.

Ray laughed. "He's not that bad."

Susan walked in on Caden's arm. "He *is* that bad." She smiled at Dean. "I hear we're planting a garden today?"

"I'm putting you to work," Dean said, handing her Bonny. "Your job is to entertain Bonny. She wants to go outside." He leaned up and kissed Ray's cheek. "I'll be outside if you need me. Please send Yeo out when you're done."

Ray watched him go, hand pressed to his tingling cheek.

"Aww," Jackson said, fluttering his eyes. "Look at the big, silent beta. He's blushing."

Ray scowled and wrapped an arm around Jackson. "Come on, guys. I have something to tell you."

"Is it about you and Papa dating? Because if it is, it's too late," Yeo said. "Zoe told everyone."

Ray sighed. "Unfortunately, that's not it."

CHAPTER 7

*D*ean hugged Yeo as they sat next to each other in the cool grass near the garden. Yeo had needed his papa after Ray finished telling them all about Michael. They watched as Susan frowned into her phone. She had insisted on continuing the planting and had said she'd watch a YouTube video about planting peas. She set her phone down and grabbed a rake.

Yeo sniffled and settled his head against Dean's chest. "What is she doing?"

"I don't know, baby," Dean said, kissing the top of his head. "We'll let her figure it out."

He gently petted Bonny to calm her down when Beau leaned over and sniffed her head. The guinea pig sat in his lap, and Beau curled up around them.

"I don't want to believe he would hurt me," Yeo said quietly. "I've written him off, you know? After finding out what he did to you, I can't even think of reconciling with him. Why is it so hard to believe he'd try to hurt me?"

"You looked up to him for most of your life, baby. That's a hard thing to let go of," Dean said.

"I don't understand how Fawn puts up with him," Yeo said. "I know she likes the money, but is it really enough?"

"Fawn already had Derek by the time she found out Michael's true nature," Dean said. He thought of the woman who had tried her best to help him. "Her family would have been mortified if she'd divorced Michael."

"What?" Yeo leaned back and looked at Dean.

"I'm not trying to make excuses for Fawn, but she had limited options and two children to think of," Dean pointed out.

"Two?"

"Derek and you," Dean said. "The day she learned about me, she called and we talked. She promised she would take care of you since I couldn't. She had two sons to care for, a family that would disown her in a heartbeat, and a father-in-law with more money and influence than anyone else she knew."

"I thought she chose to stay with him because of the money," Yeo said.

"I'm not saying that isn't part of it," Dean said. "Derek and you were her priority though."

They watched Susan tromp through the dirt, using the handle of the rake to make holes in the ground every six inches.

"What about now? What do you think Fawn will do?" Yeo asked.

They started giggling when Susan's boot stuck in the soft soil and she face-planted. Susan pushed to her knees and looked up at the sky, growling. She wiped her face off and got up, pushing on with determination.

"I think Fawn will reassess things and make a decision," Dean said. "She still has Lowell to worry about, but you and Summer are safe. Derek is an adult and isn't under his father's influence anymore." He stroked Yeo's hair back from his face. "Fawn will take care of her family, never doubt that. You have Summer, Linc, and Nari to worry about."

"I had forgotten how exhausting newborns were," Yeo said, nose scrunching up. "Nari is adorable, but she is a crying, pooping machine."

"Trust me," Dean said wryly. "Min reminded me."

"Caden and Summer adore her though," Yeo said, smiling. "Linc is withholding judgement."

"Where is everyone today?" Dean could admit that he had wanted snuggle time with his grandkids.

"Summer is at Hannah's house, Linc crashed Olive's Aunt Zoe day, and Nari is spending time with Rue at Abuela's house," Yeo said. "I am enjoying the peace and quiet and snuggling with my papa."

"I love you, baby boy," Dean said and kissed Yeo's forehead again.

"Should we help Susan?" Yeo asked as they watched her fall again.

Dean giggled again. She was so dirty. "I guess so."

THE NEXT DAY, Dean looked at his reflection in the mirror. His hair was smoothed back, and the white threads at his temples contrasted jarringly with his black hair. He sighed, then shrugged. Ray had known what Dean looked like when he'd agreed to go out with him. It was his own damn fault if Dean's age bothered him.

"Papa," Jimmy said, poking his head in the bathroom. "We picked out your outfit. Come on."

"I already picked something out," Dean said, walking into the bedroom. "Aren't you boys supposed to be getting ready to go to Jackson's house?"

"Papa," Min said, rolling over in his walker. He waved his rabbit at Dean and puckered his lips. Dean leaned down so Min could give him a sloppy kiss.

"Your outfit was boring," Jimmy said. "Jeans, Papa? Really?"

"You would look beautiful in anything, Papa," Jules said from the bed.

He sat between Beau and Lucy. Bonny sprawled on top of Beau, wearing a brand new pink tutu. The guinea pig fit right in with the rest of Dean's pets. Pounce lurked under the bed, eyes glaring at Dean.

"Thank you, Jules," Dean said, then arched a brow at Jimmy. Jeans were okay, damn it.

"You're going on your first date with Ray, Papa," Jimmy said. "We need to wow and amaze the guy, and dad jeans aren't going to work."

"We're going to the diner for a late lunch," Dean said. "Jeans are perfect."

"Oh, will you bring me back some cheese fries,

Papa?" Jake called over from where he sat with Lola and Betty in the window seat.

"Yes," Dean said with a laugh.

"Jeans are perfect, Jimmy," Jake said.

"No," Jimmy said, stomping his foot. "You are wearing slacks and the nice cashmere sweater we got you for Christmas." He glared at Dean. "You are *not* wearing your boots, Papa."

Dean gasped. "Not wear my boots? What am I supposed to wear?"

Jimmy held up a pair of brown loafers and Dean scowled.

"Loafers," he said, scathingly. "I'm supposed to wear loafers?"

"Papa is a cowboy, Jimmy," Jake said, the scowl on his face perfectly matching Dean's.

"Today, Papa is going to be a man on a date," Jimmy said firmly, handing Dean the shoes. "That means he needs to leave his stinky boots at home."

Dean and Jake both gasped in outrage. "Stinky?" Dean crossed his arms. "My boots are perfect. Ray got them for me when we first moved up here."

"Yes," Jimmy said, nodding slowly. "And you've worn them every day since then."

"Fine," Dean said and grabbed the loafers. "Slacks, sweater, and loafers." He dressed quickly, then spun around awkwardly. "Happy?"

He looked like a dork.

"Oh, Papa," Jules said, clapping. "You're so handsome."

Dean's heart melted. Damn, but he loved his boys.

"Thank you, sweetheart," Dean said. He heard his phone ringing.

Jules grabbed it from the nightstand and looked at it. He scrunched up his nose. "It's Grandpa." He held it out to Dean.

"Hello?" Dean kept his tone brisk and went back into the bathroom, shutting the door behind him.

"Dean," Fred Kirby said, voice stern. Dean's alpha father was always stern. Stern and cold.

"Father," Dean said, then stayed quiet. Fred Kirby didn't like chitchat.

"I've managed to convince a good man from my church to take on Jackson. My congregation is familiar with your hedonistic rebellion, but they understand Jackson is salvageable. You are to send Jackson to me by the weekend. Understand?"

Dean blinked and held his phone out from his ear, staring at it in disbelief. He brought it back to his head in time to hear his father's voice.

"Dean? Do you understand?"

"No," Dean said, then hung up. "I'm not even going to try to explain it."

He shook his head and left the bathroom. The boys watched him with eagle eyes.

"Was he mean?" Jake's face turned stubborn. "You don't have to listen to him anymore, Papa."

"I know, honey," Dean said, smiling. He shook his head again and rolled his eyes. "He wants to marry off Jackson."

"Uh oh," Jules said. "Jackson won't like that. He says he's going to stay single for the rest of his life."

"Well, I told him no and hung up on him," Dean said, groaning when the phone rang again. He looked at the screen and silenced it. "If you boys need me, send me a text, alright? I'm ignoring calls."

"Good," Jimmy said, biting his lip. "You don't think they'll try to marry me off, do you? You were just eighteen when they made you marry *him*."

"They can try all they want," Dean said. "You boys will marry whoever you want, whenever you want. Well, when you're adults you will. Jules, you can't marry Harry tomorrow."

"It would have been beautiful," Jules said sadly. "Petunia would be my best pig, and we'd have a pudding cake."

Dean laughed. "Come on. Let's get you boys to Jackson's house. You have movies to watch. Remember not to give Min any popcorn."

They piled into their old, rusty van and drove to town. Dean dropped them off at Jackson's house, then headed to the diner. He parked and smiled when he saw Ray's car already there.

He walked past The Book Worm and Honey Buns, then pushed open the door to The Cozy Kitchen, smiling at the jangling bell. His smile faded when he saw Ray at a table near the back with one of the diner's waitresses on his lap, kissing him. She was tall, young, and full-figured with a head full of red hair. Ray's desperate eyes met his as he tried to gently pry the woman off him. Dean saw red.

He stalked across the diner and grabbed the

woman's nasty red hair. He pulled her head back. "Get your lips off my boyfriend."

"What the fuck?" the woman screamed, yanking her hair and head out of his hands. "Watch it, asshole."

She stood, towering over Dean in her heels. Who the hell wore heels to waitress in?

"Keep your hands to yourself," he hissed. The woman, her nametag said Linda, pushed him back.

"That fine chocolate stallion is mine," Linda said, hands on her hips. "He needs a real woman, not some used-up, old omega."

Chocolate stallion? Dean gagged. "He's my date, so back off," Dean said again, trying to clear the disgusted look from his face.

The woman pushed him again, and he fell back a step. "I'll do whatever the fuck I want and you can leave. Now."

"Ma'am, I'm here with Dean. Please leave us alone," Ray said, standing behind her and wringing his hands.

"My. Date." Dean growled.

Linda pulled her arm back and aimed a punch at his face. He dodged most of it, but her fist still grazed his eye, and he knew it would be swollen in the morning.

After her first hit, the fight was on. Ray and the other diners tried to pry them apart, but Linda had freaking claws and was free with them.

Dean grabbed a handful of her hair while he dodged her knee and yanked, falling back when long strands came off. He held her extensions up as she screamed and jumped toward him with her claws extended.

He ran, dodging around the tables and chairs as she

chased him. She jumped a table, sliding across it and landed on him, bringing them both to the ground. They rolled around the floor, and Dean did his best to protect his eyes from the she-beast's claws.

"Enough," a loud voice yelled.

Linda was lifted off him and pulled away by a man in a police uniform.

Tanner, another policeman, knelt beside him. "Are you alright, Dean?"

"Dean?" Ray's worried face appeared over his. "Baby, I am so sorry. It's all my fault. I told her I was waiting on my date, and she just sat on me and kissed me."

"It's true, man." Another man's face appeared above him. This was someone Dean didn't know, but he wore a cook's apron. "Linda has a serious crush on your man, here. She didn't listen to a word he said."

"That's not your fault, Ray," Dean said, wincing. His lip was split. "No means no."

"Oh, damn. You've got scratches all over," Ray said, helping him sit up.

Dean groaned as his leg told him he was too damn old to be fighting over a man.

Dean held up the red extensions. He handed it to Ray. "I feel like I should present this to you, then pee on your leg."

Tanner groaned and covered his face as the cook laughed.

Ray grinned. "No need for that. I'm yours, cowboy."

"You're going to have to come down to the station," Tanner said. "We have plenty of witnesses saying she started it, and Gib here isn't going to press charges for the damages to the restaurant, right?"

Tanner looked at the cook.

"No way, man," Gib said. "My mama sure would have but I own the family diner now, so you're good. I'm sorry one of my employees attacked you. If it helps any, her ass is fired."

"Will you give her back her hair?" Dean held out the extensions.

CHAPTER 8

*R*ay slid low in his chair as Gramps paced back and forth, fuming. Carter and Juan sat on either side of him, and Noah worked on getting drinks from the soda machine. Caden was with Yeo at the moment, so all of Ray's friends had insisted on being with him.

"How dare they keep Dean like this?" Gramps growled.

"He did get into a fight, Gramps," Ernie said.

Ray's friend slid down in his chair when Gramps turned to glare at him.

"They're just questioning him," Susan said. Dean's best friend was perfectly calm and collected. She typed a text on her pone. "John is with him and won't let anything happen to him."

"Hey guys," Tanner said, sitting across from them.

"Tanner, you go get Dean right now." Gramps stood in front of the man, arms crossed, and scowled.

"Gramps, I can't do that," Tanner said, sliding low in his own chair.

Yeah, they all knew how he felt. Gramps had already yelled at him for not taking care of Linda himself. Ray hadn't wanted to hit a woman, but Gramps was right. He should have done more.

"They're almost finished, and then Dean is free to go. We aren't charging him with anything," Tanner said.

"What about that horrible woman?" Susan arched a perfect brow.

"Gib and Dean both don't want to press charges. She'll get a warning and everyone will go home. Well, after the EMT finishes up with Dean."

"What! Is he hurt? She scratched him up pretty bad," Ray said. His own arms had long scratches from where he'd tried to pry her off Dean.

"He's okay," Tanner said. "He has a busted lip, black eye, scratched face, neck, and arms, and a sprained wrist."

"That's not okay," Grammy said angrily from her seat next to Susan.

"Everyone," Susan said, holding her hand up. "If this were, say, Abel, would you all be so upset?"

"I'm not dating Abel," Ray said.

Susan waved him away. "Not you, Ray. I mean Gramps and Grammy."

"Well," Grammy said, blinking. "I don't want any of my kids or grandkids hurt."

"If it were Abel, you would be rolling your eyes and lecturing him on staying out of drama," Susan said.

"This is Dean," Gramps said. "He's been through so much this week alone. First that bastard at Noah's place and now this."

"He handled it," Susan said. "John has been texting me and Dean is just fine." She leaned forward in her seat, face triumphant. "Think about it."

"Oh," Grammy said and covered her mouth when she gasped. "He didn't have a panic attack."

"It might have been because she's a woman so he wasn't triggered, but it's still progress," Noah said.

Susan stood and paced before them like a general. "When he comes out of there, Gramps, you lecture him as if he were Abel." She looked at Ray. "You treat him like he just won your hand in a joust."

"Aww," Juan, grinning.

"You two," Susan said, shooting Juan and Carter a look.

They sat up, ready for their orders.

"Feel free to give him shit," she said.

Carter gasped. "Mother. Language."

"It's all that manual labor she does with Dean," Noah said, shaking his head. "It brings out her inner cowboy."

Ernie laughed. "She even has calluses on her hands. I saw them."

The doors to the station flew open and all of Dean's kids came in. Caden pushed Nari in her stroller and had his rabbit, Huckleberry, riding in a baby sling across his chest. Yeo held Linc's hand and went straight to Tanner.

"Where's my Papa?"

"Calm down, guys," Ray said, jumping up. They all turned worried faces to him. "He's fine and will be out in a minute or two." He smiled at the boys and took Min from Jackson. "Don't give him too hard a time, alright?"

"What happened?" Jules's lip trembled.

Ray about broke then and there. These boys had been through so much and didn't need to have to worry about their papa being attacked by jealous waitresses. Ray thought about what Susan said.

"He had to fight to protect my honor," Ray said, giving a big, drawn-out sigh.

Jules giggled and hugged Ray while Jake snorted and started laughing.

"What does that mean?" Jimmy crossed his arms and looked at Ray suspiciously.

Ray stifled his smile and patted Min on the back. "There I was, minding my own business, and sitting in the diner waiting for your papa to get there. Then *she* came to the table."

"Who?" Jake said, sitting next to Grammy.

She wrapped her arm around the boy's shoulders and winked at Ray.

"Linda," Carter and Juan said together, voices full of gloom.

By the time they brought Dean out, the boys were rolling with laughter, even Yeo and Jackson.

"What's going on out here?" Dean looked rough, but his smile was bright and reassuring.

John and Hobson Hills's sheriff stood behind him.

The sheriff nodded to Gramps and Grammy, and John pulled Susan to her feet and kissed her cheek.

"Papa," Min said, waving. He laid his head against Ray's chest and sleepily rubbed his face against Ray's shirt. "Dada."

"Papa," Jules said, jumping up and down. "Ray said you had to fight for his honor." He wrapped his arms around Dean's waist. "Did you really roll around on the diner floor?"

Dean winced. "I did." He stood beside Ray and looked at his sons. "Don't go getting ideas. My date would have gone a lot better without any fighting."

"Linda was attacking Ray with her icky lips," Jake said, shaking his head. "You needed to protect him." He gave his dad a worshiping look. "Sometimes you have to stand up and protect your people, Papa. It's what cowboys do."

Ray tried to hide another smile, but failed miserably.

"Well, your papa here can go home now," Sheriff McKenzie said. He looked at the boys. "Fighting isn't a good thing, but you boys are right. Your papa needed to help his boyfriend and defend himself." He patted Dean on the back. "You did good, son. Next time, just give us a call though, alright?"

"No more catfights for me," Dean agreed, nodding. He hugged Jules and leaned into Ray's side. "Home?"

"Definitely," Ray said, wrapping an arm around Dean and Jules. "Pizza and a movie?"

"That sounds perfect," Dean said.

"I'll pick up some pizzas on the way to the house,"

Jackson said and kissed his papa's cheek. "You know we're crashing your date now." He pried Jules from Dean and headed out the door along with Jake and Jimmy.

"All of us," Yeo said and picked up Linc. "We'll grab a bunch of movies from the house and be right behind you guys."

Ray couldn't make himself release Dean. His omega felt so good against his side and in his arms.

Gramps and Grammy came to stand in front of them, and Dean bowed his head. "I'm so sorry I embarrassed you all. Sheriff McKenzie knew we were connected and insisted on calling you."

"Would have had to do that for any of Gerard's kids," the sheriff said.

"Gerard? Who's Gerard?" Carter looked around the room as if another person would pop up.

"That's me," Gramps said, snickering. He grabbed Carter and pushed him toward the door.

Juan snorted. "Okay, who here knew Gramps's first name?"

Grammy and the sheriff were the only ones who raised their hands.

"Really, Noah and Ernie? He's your grandpa," Juan said.

Noah shrugged. "It's always just been Gramps."

"Maybe I knew?" Ernie's face squished up as he thought hard, then cleared when he shrugged. "Nope. Didn't know."

Grammy ignored them and hugged Dean. "Oh, Dean. We're not embarrassed by you at all, though we do have something to say about brawling with waitresses in the diner, young man."

"That's right, Dean," Gramps said sternly. "We need to have a talk about using your words."

Ray could almost forget the man's earlier panic. Almost.

Dean gave them both a wide-eyed look. "Okay?"

"This one is a lot more sensible than your other kids, Gerard," Sheriff McKenzie said.

He patted Dean on the back again and waved them all out the door. Ray carried Min to Dean's van. Juan had fetched the cars from the diner as they waited for Dean to be released.

"I'll follow in Dean's car," Susan said. "John and I will be joining you for your movie night." She stroked Dean's cheek. "Oh, sweetheart, you look horrible."

"Thanks," Dean said dryly.

"Don't complain. For once, it's you and not me. We'll fix you up at home," Susan said and grabbed Ray's keys from his hand.

Ray drove toward the house with Min in his car seat in the back, a car seat Ray had bought *just in case*. Ray grinned as he thought about how much he had changed his life to suit Dean and the kids over the past year. Yet Juan and Carter still hadn't known he was pining. Elijah was right. The two men were oblivious.

"I'm really sorry about what happened," Ray said, breaking the comfortable silence. "That woman has been flirting with me for a while, but I've always just ignored her."

"It's not your fault, Ray," Dean said. He bit his lip,

then winced. "You're a handsome man and a lot of people in town chase after you. I see it every time we go out." Dean snickered. "Min usually chases them off, though, no fighting needed. I really need to try to get him to call you by your name."

"I should be honest," Ray said. "I *may* have been the one who taught Min to call me dada."

"Ray!"

"I know, I know," Ray said. "He's my baby boy though. You're his papa and I'm his dada. That's how it should be." Ray blushed, happy his dark skin made it hard to see. "I've belonged to you the second we met, so the men and women in town can chase me all they want, but I'm already taken."

"Oh, Ray," Dean said. He leaned his head back against the seat. "I've never had someone of my own. I'll treasure you. I promise. Are you sure though? I'm forty-six and the doctor that delivered Jules said I'd never have kids again. You could do so much better."

"You're not just a baby machine, Dean," Ray said, mad that the only value Dean gave himself was for breeding. "You're a strong, sweet man with a huge heart. I love that I have to drag you inside when it's raining or snowing because you love the outdoors so much. You think you're weak, but I know how strong you are. I see how much you love your sons. You're a beautiful person, and I would be perfectly happy to be by your side for the rest of my life, any way you'll have me."

"Ray," Dean said, tears trickling down his face. "That's... really? That's how you see me?"

"Yeah," Ray said. "We've been friends for a while now, right? Now we're going to be more." He shook his head and smiled softly, wondering why he'd been so afraid. "You and me fit together, don't we?"

"We do," Dean said quietly. "I wish we had both pulled our heads out of our asses sooner."

Ray laughed. "Me too." He glanced over at Dean. His omega watched him with dark, wet eyes. "I was stuck up on you being an omega. My stepdad had ideas about what a real man was. For a long time, I tried to fit his image of the perfect beta. He thought betas were meant to be grunts."

"What?" Dean frowned. "Why would he think that?"

"Some people get caught up in tradition and can't think for themselves. Maybe he had his own reasons. I don't know," Ray said, shrugging. He continued. "He thought betas were meant to work hard, not think too much, and follow orders. That's why I joined the army. I hate violence, but I wanted to be a *real* beta." Ray cringed. "My stepdad also thought betas should only date and marry either women or other betas, because alphas and omegas were meant for each other."

"That's stupid," Dean said, then snorted. "All of it is. You're so smart, smarter than a lot of alphas I know. He must have hated that."

Ray laughed again. "He really did."

"This is really why you didn't make a move sooner?" Dean's expression told Ray exactly what he thought of it.

"That is the biggest reason," Ray admitted. "I didn't want to risk our friendship or make you uncomfortable either, but yeah, I'm an idiot. I had this idea that you would meet some wonderful alpha and fall in love."

"So you taught Min to call you dada," Dean said, giggling. "That's so passive aggressive."

His giggles turned to laughter and Ray joined him.

An hour later, a freshly showered and bandaged Dean curled into Ray on the couch. The living room was full and *The Princess Bride* played on the television. The smell of pizza and breadsticks filled the air, and Ray had to admit that this was the best date he'd ever had.

CHAPTER 9

*T*wo weeks later, Dean and Ray finally got to go on a date by themselves. Dean loved his kids, but they hogged Ray.

The Irish Rose was busy for a Sunday afternoon, and Dean had to fight the urge to hide his face. His nerves about being seen in public were much better than a year ago, but he still found himself struggling occasionally. Ray's hand on his lower back sent confidence rushing through him as Ray led him to a table near the back.

"This place is really busy," Ray said.

"Justin and Abel hired a great cook a month ago," Dean said, sitting. "Pub food is trendy now." He picked up a menu and looked it over. "Oh, I love chicken salad."

"I'm just surprised there are so many families here," Ray said, looking around.

Dean looked up and followed Ray's gaze. There really were quite a few families having lunch. He saw

Justin at the bar and waved. The young omega smiled and came over, bringing two ice waters with him.

"No fights allowed here, Dean," Justin said with a wink.

"I'll try to restrain myself," Dean said wryly. "How's business?"

"Really good," Justin said. "Between the tourists and our locals, we stay busy. I'm going to have to hire another bartender soon."

Justin looked back at the line at the bar, then leaned down and hugged Dean. "Crap. I'll see you guys later. Rhea will be over to get your order."

He rushed back to the bar and a young woman moved to stand next to their table. They both ordered and she left, giving them privacy.

"Yeo texted me this morning to complain about his *guards*," Dean said, snickering. "He said West and Cullen were teaching Summer how to kill a man seventy-eight ways."

Ray laughed. "Hort said they were enjoying their time here way too much." He winced. "I wish the FBI would finish this so Yeo didn't have to worry so much. It kills me that Cook and Vandenburg aren't concerned at all. They're just going about their lives while Yeo's is put on hold."

"It'll come to a head soon enough. It doesn't really surprise me that Michael and his friend don't seem worried," Dean said. "Fawn and I spoke often over the years and the sheer arrogance that man has is unbelievable." Dean made a face. "Let's talk about something else."

Ray smiled nervously. "Okay. Um, so, I talked to Shawn about that Nissan. He has it all fixed up and ready to sell."

"You bought it, didn't you?" Dean arched a brow and watched Ray squirm in his seat.

"I thought maybe I could give it to Jimmy for his birthday in October," Ray said.

"You're really going to wait that long to give it to him?" Dean tilted his head. "I don't believe you."

"Tell me what I can do," Ray said, eyes pleading. "Jimmy needs a car."

"How much was it?"

"Twenty-five hundred. Shawn knew it was for Jimmy and insisted on knocking a lot off the price. Basically, he just charged me for the parts it took to fix it."

"Okay," Dean said. "I'll pay for half, and we'll give it to him as a birthday present from the both of us." He gave Ray a hard look. "You can't buy him anything else for his birthday. Understand?"

Ray grimaced. "I don't know if I can promise that. I already got him a bunch of art supplies."

"It's March," Dean said, exasperated. "Okay, then. Nothing else besides what you already got."

"If you insist," Ray said, sighing heavily. He grinned at Dean. "I love your kids. You know that right?"

"I've suspected for a while," Dean said, giggling as he remembered coming home to find Ray helping Jimmy dye his streaks purple. Beau had tried to help and now Dean's golden retriever had an edgier look.

"I've been meaning to ask you about Drew's friend, Terry. Did you ever find them?"

"I went the legal route and talked to the social worker that works with Bennett," Ray said. "She found them and checked in. They're living with a really nice foster family and got to talk to Drew and his family a few days ago."

Dean smiled and propped his chin on his fist. "My hero."

Ray laughed. "I wish all my jobs were that nice." He took Dean's free hand in his own. "Jimmy mentioned your dad called a couple weeks ago. Are you having trouble with him?"

"He's called a few times trying to convince me to force Jackson to marry some guy from his church," Dean said, scowling. "I've been very clear with him each time. My boys are going to pick their own spouses. Besides, Jackson is bisexual, like you. He may fall in love with a woman. Who knows? Omegas don't *have* to marry alphas."

"I'm sorry you have to deal with that," Ray said.

"I'm used to it. Not every Christian in Jackson is like my dad, but you know how your stepdad had ideas about proper betas? My dad has ideas about proper omegas. Luckily, I'm the only omega they had. My other two brothers are alphas."

"What about your papa?"

Dean smiled sadly. "I don't know really. He was so browbeaten by the time I was born. I remember having fun and being happy when we were alone. Then my dad or my brothers would get home and we would basically turn into servants."

"Do you ever get to talk to him?"

"No," Dean said, sitting up when Rhea set their food and drinks in front of them. She left them to eat and Dean dipped his fry in mustard. "Dad doesn't let him talk to anyone. I think if I called during the day, I might get to speak to him, but he could get in trouble for it. Dad's idea is that an omega is easily led astray and needs a firm hand and guidance. Simon felt the same way. His hand was just a little rougher than Dad's."

"You worry about him," Ray said, making a face when Dean dunked another fry in his mustard.

"Don't judge my mustard love," Dean said, laughing. Then he sighed and shrugged. "To answer your question, I do worry about Papa. I've been exactly where he is. I truly thought if I left Simon, he would get the kids. Then he would hurt them. I never knew there were resources out there for omegas like me. Papa was in an even worse state when he married my dad. He was raised in a really traditional family in South Korea. My dad arranged the marriage with his parents, then changed Papa's name as soon as he arrived in Tennessee. He gave him a good, American name and made him learn English."

Dean made a face and dunked another fry.

"Your dad sounds so charming," Ray said.

"Right?" Dean took a big bite of his sandwich.

His parents' marriage was a lot like Dean and Simon's. He wished things had been different, but no one could change the past. All he could do now was make sure his kids had a better life. He swallowed and took a drink of his green beer.

"What about you and your stepdad? Do you guys still talk," Dean asked.

"Nope," Ray said and gave a surprising smile.

Dean hummed happily. He loved Ray's smile. So much bright kindness.

"He got pissed when I didn't re-enlist with the army. I haven't missed him a bit."

"What about your mom?"

"She does what he says. Always has," Ray said, shrugging. "My parents got divorced when I was three, so I don't even really remember my dad. He started a new family and Mom married Douchebag a few months later." He looked thoughtful. "I really thought I would miss them more, but then Carter called needing help and I ended up moving here. I learned a while ago that blood doesn't make family. Hell, Gramps and Grammy have been better parents in the time I've been here than my own were my whole life."

"Gerard and Laurel," Dean said, musing.

"You enjoy knowing their names, don't you?" Ray laughed at him.

"I've gone months without knowing," Dean said, flushing. "I still call them Gramps and Grammy, but it's nice to actually know their names."

They finished eating and waved to Justin as they left.

Dean leaned into Ray. "Where to next, hero?"

Ray slid an arm around his waist and walked him to the car. "I know a place I think you'll like."

He helped Dean into the car and they drove out of town.

"Where are we going?"

"You'll see," Ray said, laughing.

There was still snow on the ground despite the warmer spring weather, but Hobson Hills was starting to come alive with green. They drove for a while, then Ray pulled over.

"Gramps told me about this little spring house. There's a covered bridge too," he said.

Dean smiled softly. Ray knew him well. He got out, happy he had worn his boots and coat. They walked through the trees for a few minutes, then came across a faded red-covered bridge.

"Ray, this is beautiful." Dean rushed forward, only limping a bit. The bridge covered a large, fast-moving creek. He looked across the dark bridge. "Can we cross it?" He glanced back over his shoulder.

Ray carried a basket and a folded blanket in one arm. "Yeah," Ray said. "The spot we want is right across the bridge." He took Dean's hand. "Come on."

They walked for a few minutes, crossing the bridge and coming to an old, crumbling spring house. The structure was mostly standing and it was clean inside, but the wall facing the creek had crumbled. Ray set the basket down and spread the blanket out.

Dean crawled onto the blanket and sprawled out. "What did you bring?"

He looked out at the creek and sighed happily. He really loved being outside. Ray sat beside him and pulled out a bottle of fancy juice and two glasses.

"We don't need to drink anymore after that beer with lunch, but I brought us some juice."

He poured them both a glass and they clinked them together before grinning at each other and draining their glasses.

"How is it going with Dr. Woodward?"

"Surprisingly good. We talk once a week and probably will for a long time. It's tough to talk about what happened with Michael and Simon, but it's cathartic somehow. I may always have flashbacks and nightmares, but I won't let those memories control my life. I want to live and be happy." Dean breathed in the clean air, enjoying the sounds of birds. "This is really nice, Ray. Thank you."

"I've wanted to show you this place since I found it. We don't usually get a lot of time to ourselves," Ray said.

"That won't change anytime soon. Are you sure you really want to be with me? It can't be easy."

"It's easy because I love you," Ray said, then froze. "Shit. Did I say that out loud?"

"Ray," Dean said, shocked.

He set his glass down and leaned into the beta, bringing their lips together. Ray's lips were warm and parted for Dean. Ray moaned, then pulled Dean to him, deepening the kiss. Before he knew it, Dean was in Ray's lap, wrapped up in his arms. He felt like he was on fire and his trembling fingers worked on Ray's shirt.

"Dean," Ray said roughly. "Are you sure about this?"

"Yes," Dean said, hissing. "I want you, Ray. More than anything in the world."

"Thank god," Ray said and pulled Dean down, settling him onto the blanket.

Ray kissed him again while his hands roamed across Dean's body. He slowly undressed Dean, seeming to enjoy every bit of skin revealed. Dean knew his body didn't look bad. He worked hard every single day.

Ray hummed happily as he ran his hands over the muscles in Dean's stomach before wrapping his big hand around Dean's hard dick. He pumped him once and Dean moaned.

"I want you in me, Ray," Dean said.

"I'll get there," Ray said, smiling.

He took his time and caressed and kissed every part of Dean's body, giving plenty of attention to Dean's dick in the process.

Dean panted, sweat covering his body. His legs were spread wide and he writhed as Ray finally entered him. Ray was big and it took time to get comfortable, but Dean had never felt so full, so complete.

His eyes were locked on Ray's dark gaze as the beta moved slowly, friction sending heat shooting through Dean's body.

Ray carefully lifted Dean's sore leg, then leaned down, bracing himself on his arms above Dean. He wrapped his arms around Ray's neck and watched his face as their bodies twisted and danced together.

Ray moved faster, breathing heavily, and Dean cried out when Ray rubbed against his prostate and came, splattering against their stomachs.

His beta growled, then pounded into him, eyes fixed

on Dean's face. He came seconds later, filling Dean up with his cum.

Ray pressed his face into Dean's neck and nibbled.

"That was... that was something else, Dean." His voice was gruff and broken.

Dean pulled him close, savoring the weight of Ray's body pressing him into the blanket.

"It's never been like that," he whispered. "That was so beautiful. You inside me is better than a warm summer's day, Ray."

He felt cum trickle from his body and sadness overwhelmed him. He wished he could have Ray's baby.

"Dean?" Ray cupped his face, wiping away the tears on his cheeks. "What's wrong, cowboy?"

"I wish..." Dean started, then stopped. There was no use in wishing. Ray loved him. He knew Dean's true worth. "I love you, Ray. If you want me, I'm yours."

Ray rolled them over, laughing. "Thank god. The boys and I were planning a campaign to convince you to love me. It involved more guinea pigs and we really don't need any more pets."

CHAPTER 10

A few weeks later, Ray and Jake were feeding the animals in the barn together.

Dean had only let Ray go to his apartment to get some clothes. Since their time at the spring house, he'd insisted Ray sleep beside him every night. Ray hadn't complained. The boys had handled it well, accepting his presence without question.

Ray took a minute and patted Jackie's nose while Jake crooned to his mare, Dottie. The boy didn't look a thing like his papa, but Ray swore they were just alike.

"Can we go for a ride this weekend?" Jake asked. "I haven't gotten to ride Dottie for a while because of the weather." He moved to the next stall and scratched El Paso's ear. "Papa gets to ride El Paso for work all the time. It's not fair."

"Well, you can't ride a horse to school," Ray said, smiling as he pictured Dottie tied to the bicycle rack at the high school. "We'll go for a ride this weekend." He looked around to make sure Jules and Jimmy weren't close by. "Don't tell anyone, but I've never ridden a horse."

"Really?" Jake's eyes were disbelieving. "Aren't you from Texas?"

Ray winced. "Yeah, I know. It's shameful."

"It's okay," Jake said. "I'll teach you to ride on Dottie. She's really gentle. When you're ready, you can ride Gouda. She's pretty good too." Dottie whinnied and Jake rushed back to her. "Not as good as you, Dottie. I swear."

"You sure I can't ride Jackie, here?"

Jake blinked. "Well, I guess. He's trained for riding." He started giggling. "You would rather ride a donkey than a horse?"

Ray gasped and covered Jackie's big ears. "Don't listen to him, Jackie-boy. You're just as good as any horse."

The donkey brayed and leaned his head against Ray's chest.

"You're going to learn to ride on Jackson?" Jules and Petunia popped up beside Ray, making him jump.

"Good god, where were you, boy?" Ray asked, his hand pressed to his chest.

Petunia oinked and snuffled around his boots.

Jules hugged him, pressing his face into Ray's side. "It's okay, Ray. Jake is a great teacher. He and Papa taught me how to ride, and you can ride Jackson if you want. He's a good donkey."

"Papa and Mini-boo won't be home for another couple of hours," Jimmy said from Ray's other side. "Why don't you get started now?"

"Seriously. Where did you boys come from?" Ray scowled.

"Eavesdropping is the best way to learn what's going on," Jimmy said. "For example, this morning, Papa was talking to Min and I heard him say that he loved you and didn't want you to ever leave."

Ray blushed. Jake gagged and leaned over like he was going to throw up. Jules clapped, then hugged Ray again.

"Your papa and I love each other." Ray shrugged. "I have no plans to leave as long as he wants me here."

"I'm calling you dad," Jules said happily, dancing around in circles. "Then, when we cook dinner together, it won't just be Ray and me cooking dinner. It'll be my dad and me cooking dinner. You make the best Jedi when we play too. This is perfect."

He hugged Ray again, squealing. Ray blinked away his tears and hugged the boy back.

"Come on," Jake said, rolling his eyes. "It's time to teach Dad to ride. If you insist on riding a donkey, then we'll just start you out on him. Jackson really is well trained."

Ray sniffed and wiped his eyes. "Okay. Let's do this."

"Jules and I can milk the cows and get the eggs," Jimmy said, prying Jules off Ray. "We need to move your stuff into the house too, Dad. Maybe we can move you in on Saturday, then go riding Sunday." He leaned down and put a giggling Jules over his shoulder. "Come on, giggle monster. We have work to do."

Petunia huffed in indignation and followed close behind him, grunting her disapproval at their shenanigans. Daisy and Dandy popped their heads out of their hidey-hole to watch.

Ray cleared his throat, then looked at Jake. The boy grinned wide, his blue eyes wet too.

"Teach me, wise one." Ray bowed his head toward Jake. His new son laughed, then grabbed his hand, tugging him toward the tack room.

"THEN, Susan and I decided that maybe a knitting club isn't for us," Dean said. They sat at the kitchen table, eating dinner. "We really like seeing everyone there, but all they do is sit in chairs and knit things."

"What did you think a knitting club was?" Ray chuckled when he noticed the boys were as confused as him.

"I don't know," Dean said, shrugging. "I thought we'd talk about harvesting hair from sheep and rabbits or something like that."

Jimmy laughed. "Did Susan think that too?"

Dean scowled. "No. She knew it was boring. She thought she would be better at it though. Turns out, she's worse at knitting than Grey."

"They have a gardening club in town, don't they?" Ray thought he had heard Grammy talking about that at some point.

"I would like that," Dean said, looking thoughtful. "Susan didn't do too bad planting peas either."

Ray wasn't sure Susan would agree with that assessment. By the time John brought the boys back,

C.W. GRAY

she had been exhausted and covered in dirt. His phone rang, pulling him from his thoughts.

"I should take this," he said, looking at the number. "It's Hort."

Dean's phone rang from the counter, and Dean got up to check it. "Yeo?"

Ray ducked into the living room and answered. "Hey, Hort."

"Has Yeo told you what happened?" Hort's tone was brisk.

"He's on the phone with Dean now," Ray said. "What's going on?"

"Richard Cook called him and made threats. We have the phone records and I've listened to the conversation. The fucker threatened to kill Yeo's sister, son, and daughter in graphic detail," Hort said. The man sounded pissed. "He pushed for Yeo to come back to the company and remarry his ex-wife. He offered him everything, even after he threatened him. The man's behavior is completely erratic, which is worrying."

"That asshole," Ray said, teeth clenched. "What did Yeo say?"

Ray could hear a smile in Hort's voice. "Yeo said that he had a home here with his real family. He said his husband and children had plenty of protection, and he had his father and brothers with him. He ended the conversation by saying that there was nothing that Richard could offer him that would be better than what he already had, then hung up on the bastard. Your soon-to-be stepson stayed calm and cool. You should be proud."

"My soon-to-be stepson?" Ray smiled.

"West told me all about your cowboy, Ray," Hort said. "I didn't even think Maine had cowboys."

"Where there are cows, there will always be cowboys," Ray said solemnly.

"Aren't they called cattle? Wait, you should know this, Ray. You're from Texas," Hort said.

"Yeah, the city of Dallas in Texas. I never met a cow until I moved here." He heard Dean's raised voice. "I better go calm Dean down. He hates it when one of the boys gets upset."

He said goodbye and ended the call.

Dean's face was red, and the boys were staring at their papa with worry. "Yeo, I love you so much. Those people don't know what they've lost, and I hope they all go to jail."

Ray sat the table and the boys looked at him.

"What's wrong?" Jimmy asked.

"We weren't going to say anything, but it's too late for that now," Ray said. "I'll tell you when you papa finishes with Yeo. Alright?"

"Is somebody hurt?" Jules asked in a small voice.

"No," Ray said. "Everyone is okay."

Dean turned back to the table and saw his sons. Ray smiled encouragingly, but Dean's anger drained and his face turned ashen.

He said goodbye to Yeo and sat in Ray's lap, tucking his head under Ray's chin. Ray wrapped his arms around his omega.

"We need to tell the boys," Ray said.

"You're right." Dean sighed. "Yeo's father and grandfather are mad at him. They have some very mean friends and threatened to hurt Yeo, Summer, Linc, and Nari. The police are going to stop them, but it takes time to gather evidence."

"Is that why West and Cullen are staying with them?" Jake asked. "They're nice and all, but I thought it was kind of weird."

"Yes," Ray said, nodding. "My boss, Hort, sent them to make sure Yeo doesn't get hurt. They work for the same company as me."

"Okay," Jimmy said, looking better, then fed Min another bite of his dinner. "I'm glad you're moving in with us, Dad. I don't like the idea of you all alone."

Dean looked up at him, eyes sparkling with joy. "Moving in? Dad?"

"We talked today, Papa," Jules said. "We decided that Ray is our dad, and he needs to live here so you'll be super happy forever. You can dance every night and he won't have to leave. I hated it when he left before."

"What does Ray say about that?" Dean looked at him, dark eyes shining.

"Ray says *hell yes*. I love you and the boys, Dean. The past few weeks have been the happiest of my life, even with the trouble with the Cooks."

"Perfect," Dean said, leaning into him. "When can we move you in?"

"We need to eat dinner first, Papa," Jules said, stuffing a spoonful of mashed potatoes in his mouth. "Don't rush us."

"Don't talk with your mouth full, baby boy," Dean said. "I'll take off early tomorrow and help Ray move. He'll be settled in by the time you guys get home from school."

Later that night, Ray sat in bed, his laptop in his lap, while Dean showered. Beau stretched along the other side of the bed and Lucy was curled up on Dean's pillow.

Pounce sprawled against Ray's leg. The grumpy cat apparently only liked Jules and Ray and alternated who he slept with. Dean hadn't been thrilled. Bonny chittered from her cage in front of the window and Pounce raised his head and hissed.

"Be nice, grumpy cat," Ray said, stroking the cat's back.

Dean's phone rang and Ray leaned over to grab it, looking at the number.

"I think 'Alphahole' probably means it's his dad," Ray told Pounce. He thought for a second, then answered. "Hello?"

"Who... who is this," a quiet voice asked. Definitely not Dean's dad.

"My name is Raymond Potts. I'm Dean's boyfriend. Is this his papa? I'm sorry, but he never actually told me your name."

"My name is Peter. I'm Dean's omega father. May he speak with me?"

"Oh," Ray said. "Yeah, he probably wants to talk to you, but he's in the shower. Hold on and I'll get him."

"That's alright," Peter said quickly. "I don't want to be a bother."

"You're his papa. You would never be a bother to him or me. Your husband, on the other hand, is a pain in the ass, but you're okay." He set his computer aside and dislodged Pounce before getting out of the bed. "Is everything okay with you? Do you need anything?"

"Me? I'm alright," Peter said awkwardly. "Fred isn't happy with Dean."

"I'm getting Dean now and you can talk with him, but Peter, I want you to know that you can call me anytime if you need something. Can I give you my number?"

"Um, okay," Peter said. "I can remember telephone numbers really well. You can tell me."

Ray gave him his number, then knocked on the bathroom door. "Dean, sweetheart. Your papa is on the phone."

"Coming," Dean said and the shower cut off.

"By the way, do you prefer Peter or your Korean name? Granted, I don't know your Korean name, but you could tell me if that's what you would prefer to go by," Ray said.

"You would do that?" Surprise filled Peter's voice. "You couldn't in front of Fred."

"I can be discrete, if it's what you want," Ray said softly.

"Min-jun," he said. "My name is Min-jun."

"Min-jun?" Ray smiled. "Well, that explains why Dean named our youngest Min."

"He did that? For me?" Min-jun sounded so shocked, and Ray wanted to reach through the phone and hug the man. "Wait. He had another baby?"

Dean opened the door, still damp and flushed from the shower. "Let me hand you over to him. He'll tell you all about it."

Dean took the phone and started talking to his papa, so Ray headed back to the bed, settling down again with his laptop and Pounce.

He pulled up Cook's file and looked through it again. The FBI were tearing apart Cook Enterprises, but there was a lot of nastiness in Michael Cook. He had hurt a lot of people and still managed to keep his position in society.

He scrolled through, looking for Richard's name. The fucker had threatened Yeo. He may not be involved in the FBI's investigation, but he wouldn't walk away clean. Not if Ray had anything to say about it.

CHAPTER 11

*A*few days later, Dean cleaned out El Paso's stall. El Paso watched from the open door to the pasture. The stinker carried Dean's stolen hat in his mouth and softly nickered at the pigs running around in his stall.

Petunia, Daisy, and Dandy tried to help Dean clean by circling him and following his every move. It wasn't working too well. He knew Beau and Lola were around there somewhere, but the dogs were better behaved than the piggies and knew how to stay out of the way.

Dean thought about his conversation with his papa as he shoveled poop. Dean's papa had called to warn Dean about the man Fred wanted Jackson to marry.

He had told Dean that the man was like Simon and begged him to stand firm. Dean had told him he would and thanked him. Then he'd told him all about Min and Yeo and his life in Hobson Hills. Dean had never thought he could be this happy, this complete. His papa had cried.

Afterwards, Ray had spoken to his papa again. Dean's beta called his papa Min-jun. If he hadn't already loved Ray, he would have fallen right then and there.

Ray had told Min-jun that they were there for him if he needed help getting away from Fred. Dean didn't think Min-jun would leave Fred, but he wished he had made it clear to his papa before that he was more than welcome in Dean's home.

He shoveled the last of the soiled straw into the wheelbarrow, then set the shovel aside and pushed the wheelbarrow toward the barn door. The compost pile was a distance from the house and barn, so he usually waited until the wheelbarrow was full before making the trip.

He came to a stop, dropping the handles on the wheelbarrow, when he saw a large man standing in the door of the barn. Dean didn't recognize him.

"Can I help you?" Dean turned his body a bit, bending as if he were looking at the wheel of the wheelbarrow.

He got his phone from his pocket and dialed Ray. He didn't like the looks of this guy. Ray was on his way home with Min after checking in with Yeo, and Dean hoped he got home soon.

"Dean Wagner?" The man's voice was close, and Dean shot up, realizing he was walking towards him.

"Yes?"

"I have a message from an old friend of yours," the man said, his smile open and friendly. "He says you need to remember your place and stop interfering with his family."

Dean squeaked and dropped the phone when he noticed the man carried a bat.

"He wants me to make sure you feel it for a while." The man swung the bat, hitting Dean in the knee of his sore leg. Dean cried out, crumpling.

The next swing was to his head.

RAY ANSWERED the phone and frowned when he just heard Dean breathing. He pulled into the driveway and looked toward the barn. The doors were wide open, which was unusual.

Then he heard the man over the phone. "I have a message from an old friend of yours."

Ray punched the gas and swerved into the grass, driving toward the barn.

"Hold on Mini-boo," he said, trying to keep the panic from his voice. "Your papa needs us."

He stopped next to the doors, cursing when he heard Dean's cries. He put the truck in park, then jumped out, running to the barn.

Before he could reach it, a large man came flying through the door, landing a good ten feet from the barn. El Paso came tearing through the door, followed by Beau and Petunia. The animals headed straight toward the scrambling man.

Ray growled and joined them. The man got to his feet, but El Paso knocked him down again, and Beau latched onto his leg. Petunia bit down on the man's arm.

When he reached him, Ray pulled the man up and shook him. "What did you do?"

"What the fuck, man! Get these monsters off me. The idiot omega won't die or anything," the man said.

Ray pulled back and hit him, fist straight to the jaw. One more punch and the man was out, sliding to the ground.

"Dean." Ray ran toward the barn. Petunia followed, but Beau sat and watched the unconscious man, growling steadily.

Dean was crumpled on the ground next to the wheelbarrow.

El Paso stood above him, snorting and stomping his back hoofs. Lola, Dandy, and Daisy lay around him and looked up when he knelt beside them.

"Oh, fuck. Dean, baby. It's going to be okay."

There was a bloody bat next to him, and his phone was right behind the wheelbarrow. Ray grabbed it and hung up, then dialed 911. Dean would be okay. He *had* to be okay.

Everything hurt.

Dean slowly woke up, a steady beeping filling the air. He felt heavy and numb, but his eyes fluttered and opened.

Daylight streamed through the blinds on the window. The walls were white, and Dean blinked again. His walls were brown. Susan and Barry had called the color something fancy, but it reminded Dean of peanuts.

"Dean? Sweetheart?" That was Ray. His man.

Ray's voice was full of tears and Dean didn't like it. No one should ever make Ray cry. He looked to his right and there stood his beta.

Ray looked a mess. His face was haggard and his clothes rumpled. He cuddled Min with one arm and held Dean's hand with his other.

"Where am I?" His voice was a croak and he noticed his throat was scratchy and dry.

"The hospital. Cook sent a man to hurt you," Ray said. "I'm so glad to see your eyes, cowboy."

"How long have I been out?"

He started taking note of his body. His left arm was in a cast and his bum leg was wrapped up. His face felt swollen and he hurt all over.

"Just over twelve hours," Ray said. "You had a concussion and the doctors were really worried."

"I'll be okay, hero," Dean said. "I promise. I knew you would come get me."

Ray cried out, face twisted in pain. "I should have been there. I wanted to kill the fucker."

He closed his eyes, shuddering.

"We didn't think he would come after me," Dean said tiredly. "There was no way to know. Are the boys alright? Did anyone try to hurt Yeo?"

"The boys are okay, just really worried. No one went after Yeo at all," Ray said. "He's upset and blames himself. I've tried to make him see that it wasn't his fault, but he's a stubborn man. Just like his papa. He was in and out of here all day, but I finally talked him into taking the boys home and watching after them. I needed my Mini-boo with me."

He kissed the baby's head.

"You need to get some sleep," Dean said, eyes trying to close on him. "I'm guessing I'll be alright, and we need to make sure you are too."

It was strange. He should be freaking out with worry. How would he work? He didn't have to pay rent or a mortgage, but there were the utilities and groceries to pay for.

He knew Ray would be beside him and would take care of him and the boys. Well, as long as Dean's sweet beta didn't worry himself to death.

Ray's laugh was hollow. "You're worrying about me? Of course you are." He closed his eyes. "Your leg is broken in several places. Your arm has two breaks. You have bruises on top of your bruises and a nasty bump on your head."

"I'll live," Dean said, squeezing Ray's hand. "Did someone get that guy? I didn't recognize him."

"El Paso, Petunia, Beau, and I took him out," Ray said. "The police took him away and the FBI is sending someone to talk to him."

"El Paso? You're lying," Dean said, huffing softly. "My big baby is too gentle."

"That big baby kicked the man's ass. Beau, Petunia, and I just kept him down," Ray said, smiling half-heartedly. "The guy has hoof prints on his broken ribs, pig and dog bites, and a broken jaw."

"Good," Dean said. "I'm sorry you had to do that. I know you hate using your strength to hurt."

"I don't regret any pain that man is going through," Ray said, shaking his head. "This is one time I was more than happy to hurt someone."

"Hello?" A man poked his head in the door. "The nurse said you were awake, Mr. Wagner. I'm Dr. Little."

Another doctor followed Dr. Little into the room.

"We're glad you're awake." Dr. Little gave Dean an overview of his injuries. "We will need to do surgery on your leg, but I wanted you awake before we began because of that concussion." He looked at the other man. "This is Dr. Richards. We found something during a blood test that was a bit concerning, and after speaking with your sons, I don't think you're aware of it. Dr. Richards?"

"Hi, Dean," Dr. Richards said, smiling. "I'm an obstetrician-gynecologist. After Dr. Little called me, we did some tests. Can you tell me about your last doctor? Your son Jackson told me that you had a hard time with your last pregnancy?"

"Yes," Dean said. "Simon didn't take me to a hospital. He never did. A doctor from my dad's church would come help me when I was in labor. Dr. Jacobs was his name. After I had Jules, he said my insides were too messed up to get pregnant again."

"Church? Sounds more like a cult. In any case, he was wrong," Dr. Richards said, face reddening. "The man was a poor excuse for a doctor from what we can tell." He took a minute and calmed himself down, then forced a smile.

"What he should have told you was that it would be very difficult for you to get pregnant again, even with an alpha. Normally, at your age and with your medical history, I would have advised you to have a hysterectomy." The doctor sighed. "He didn't tell you that though."

"When we ran our normal tests, they showed that you're pregnant, Mr. Wagner. Again, considering your medical history and the fact that your current partner is a beta, this must be a shock," Dr. Little said. "That's why I brought Dr. Richards in to talk to you."

"Pregnant?" Ray looked like he was about to faint.

"I'm pregnant?" Tears fell from the corners of his eyes. He closed them and pictured a baby with Ray's smile. Oh god. His eyes flew open. "Is the baby okay?"

"Yes," Dr. Richards said. "It's very early, but everything looks good at this point. You have options, Dean. I don't think you were given many choices in the past, and I want you to know that we will support any decision you make. If you want to keep the baby, I can tell you it will be difficult because of the damage to your omega line. However, I would be honored to be with you every step of the way. I'm a good doctor and would do my absolute best to keep you and the baby healthy. If that sounds like too much for you, abortion is an option. It's your choice, and Dr. Little and I won't judge you either way."

"Ray?" Dean looked at his beta.

"I want you, Dean. I want you healthy and happy." Ray smiled tenderly. "I won't lie. The thought of you having my baby sets my heart beating so damn fast.

You're my happiness though. I don't know that I want to risk you."

"I want to risk it," Dean said in a small voice. "I love my sons, never doubt that, but I never chose pregnancy. I never wanted a baby with either Michael or Simon even though I'm thankful that I have my sons." His eyes traveled over every inch of Ray's face. He loved him so much. "I *want* to carry your baby, Ray. It may be difficult, but you'll be there with me."

"Damn right I will," Ray said.

"Perfect," Dr. Little said kindly. "We're going to prep you for surgery on that leg. I can't promise it will be the only one, but we'll know more after this one. Once that's done, we'll keep you a few days for observation, then let you go on home."

"I'll need to see you often," Dr. Richards said. "I'll schedule our first appointment with Ray while you rest." He patted Dean's good leg. "We're going to take good care of you, Dean."

The doctors left and Ray leaned down, resting his forehead gently on Dean's. "We're having a baby."

Dean laughed, tears running down his cheeks. "Seven kids. Oh god, Ray. We're turning into Bennett and Marco."

Ray laughed. "They'll think we're challenging them."

"Papa?" Jules ran into the room, face wet from tears. "You're awake!" He ran to Dean's bed and hugged his good leg, pressing his face into the blankets. "I'm careful! See?"

"You're good, Jules," Ray said kindly.

The others followed Jules in and soon the room was filled to the brim with their family and friends.

A nurse poked her head in. "You have five minutes, then I'm going to have to enforce the two guests only rule."

"We were so worried, Papa," Jake said, voice trembling.

"I'm sorry," Yeo said, gasping. He covered his face and sobbed. "I'm so sorry."

Caden pulled him into his arms and held him as he cried.

"No, baby boy," Dean said. "It's not your fault. Michael Cook is an evil man and that's on him."

Summer stood beside Ray, eyes tortured. "If I wasn't gay, he wouldn't have done this."

"Bullshit, Summer," Dean said. "It's not your fault either. That man has done plenty of horrible things and he is the only one to blame. Imagine if you had never come here. You wouldn't have met Hannah, and Yeo wouldn't have met Caden. Nari wouldn't even exist."

Hannah hugged her from behind, and Ray wrapped his arm around the girls. "He's right. Don't take the world on your shoulders, kid."

"John and I will stay at the house with the boys while you're here, Dean," Susan said, sniffling. She patted her eyes. "El Paso, Petunia, and Beau will be treated like royalty as long as I live."

"Thanks, Susan," Dean said. He tried to smile but he was so tired, and his head hurt. "We do need to tell you all something important."

"Take your time, son," Gramps said, eyes full of

worry. "The doctor said you'll be going into surgery soon."

"I'm pregnant," he blurted out.

The room was silent while everyone stared at him in amazement. Then they all started talking at once.

"You'll be tied with Bennett and me," Marco said, grinning wide. "Damn, now we have another reason to take in another kid."

"Is it a boy or a girl," Jules demanded. "I don't know if we really need another boy, but a girl would be fun. Zoe and Olive get to paint their nails, and I want to paint *my* nails. If it's a girl, we'll get Zoe spa days."

"I thought the doctor said that would be impossible?" Jackson sounded amazed. "Of course, he was an asshole, so it shouldn't surprise me that he was a shitty doctor too."

"Carter, we need to add another addition," Caden said. "I'm thinking maybe on the other side of the kitchen. Then we could add a hallway opening into the living room."

"Papa," Yeo said hesitantly. "Do you want another baby?"

Everyone quieted and watched him.

"We're behind you, no matter what," Susan said.

Dean smiled as wide as he could with a swollen face. "Boy or girl, I want to name them Jun." He looked at Caden. "You don't need to worry about adding an addition. We can make do. It's a large house." He had a sudden thought. "Oh god. Marco, I don't know how useful I'll be with a broken leg and arm."

Marco snorted. "Don't worry about that. You're on paid leave until you're better."

"No," Dean said, shaking his head. "You have a business to run, and I'll not take advantage of your kindness. Ray makes good money and can take care of us until I'm back on my feet."

"Don't get saucy with me," Marco said, scowling. "I'll find something for you to do if you insist on working."

"Times up, folks," the nurse said from the doorway.

Dean smiled and let his eyes close. He hurt and probably looked horrible, but something good had come from this shitty day.

CHAPTER 12

*R*ay sat in the corner of the surgery waiting room, his laptop perched on his knees. It was almost two in the morning, so his group were the only ones there.

Yeo, Jackson, and Summer had insisted on staying, but Ray had managed to talk Jimmy into going with the others to Bennett's house, and Gramps and Marco had taken care of the animals before coming back to the hospital to sit with him.

Jackson leaned his head against Ray's shoulder as Susan paced the floor. The clicking of her low heels somehow soothed him. Ray and Dean weren't alone. The kids were taken care of and the pets were fed.

"Ray," Jackson said. "What are we going to do?"

"Your papa will heal, Jackson," Ray said. "I work from home and will watch over him while he gets better. No problem."

"I remember him screaming when he had Jules. It hurt so badly, and that doctor really was shit," Jackson said. "Our alpha father didn't believe omegas should have anesthesia."

"That asshole," Yeo growled.

"When Jules was coming, something was wrong, and the doctor was scared. I think he thought Papa would die," Jackson said.

"This time, Dean has me," Ray said. "I'm definitely not like that jerk. Plus, he has a kickass doctor."

"Dr. Richards was my doctor when I had Nari," Yeo said. "He's really nice."

"He was Grey and Elijah's doctor too," Caden added. "I think he even delivered Olive."

"We will do everything we can to keep Dean safe," Ray said. "I know he's not just a baby factory."

"That's all *he* saw us as," Jackson said, shuddering. "He didn't see any other purpose for an omega."

Ray set his head against Jackson's. "You know he was wrong, right? Omegas are just as valuable and worthy as any other person. We make our own damn purpose in life." He huffed, then continued. "My stepdad always said betas were to keep their heads down and take orders because we weren't smart enough to do anything else."

Carter and Juan looked at one another and started laughing. Ernie signed to Noah and they both rolled their eyes, looking amused.

"You are one of the smartest men I know," Ernie said.

"Yeah," Cullen said, chuckling. "Boss man is always bragging about you."

"Clearly your stepdad is as much of an idiot as

Jackson's alpha father was," Grammy said. She sat and took Jackson's hand. "We're all here with you, sweetheart. We'll help Dean get through this."

"There's a lot to work through too," Gramps said, rubbing his eyes. "When will they question Cook's hired man?"

"Hort said the agent should arrive in the morning," West said. The large man leaned against the wall. "They want to use this in their case since it involves Vandenburg."

Ray wasn't the only one that looked disappointed. It wasn't ideal, but it's not like they had a lot of say in the matter.

"Why aren't we happy about this?" Summer looked around the room. "That means Michael will be punished, right?"

"Federal cases aren't that simple," John said tiredly. "They want Vandenburg. Likely, they'll use this and what they've discovered investigating his company to convince Cook to turn on his friend. Cook might get fined, but if he cooperates, he won't do time."

"He'll be socially ruined," Susan said. "That's something at least." Then she shook her head angrily and stomped her foot. "No. I want his fucking head on a platter, John."

"Mother," Carter said, startled. "Language. I swear you're going to give me a heart attack."

"She's right. Social ruin isn't enough." Fawn's voice came from Ray's screen. He turned his laptop around. Dean had begged him to send Fawn his file, but Ray honestly hadn't thought she would want to get involved. She had surprised him and insisted he Skype her. Ray noticed Summer slip out of view of the screen.

"Fawn," Yeo said. He was cuddled in Caden's lap, head on his alpha's chest. "Did someone call you?"

"I asked Ray to Skype with me. Dean had his handsome fella send me some information about Michael," Fawn said.

It was early in the morning in France, but Fawn's makeup and hair were impeccable. Her mouth was pressed into a thin line and anger filled her eyes.

"This is too much. He deserves to be punished for all the people he hurt, especially Dean. That omega is the sweetest man I've ever known." She blinked away tears. "I never really thought he would hurt Yeo, and I didn't even think Dean was on his radar."

"Ready for that divorce?" John asked. "I've had the papers drawn up for a while now and Michael isn't likely to retain custody of Lowell."

Ray blinked, surprised. He hadn't realized Fawn had been talking with John.

"He turns eighteen in December," Fawn said softly. "I was going to wait until then, but I just can't. He hates Michael so much and antagonizes him every time they speak." She smiled. "He's just like Summer. My two brave rebels." She cleared her throat. "I appreciate you and Susan taking the time to talk with me, John. I'm ready to do this. I've set aside money over the years. I want to use it to help Michael's victims get justice. There were so many and they're in no position to fight him. I have enough saved to pay a good lawyer to torture that man in court for the rest of his life, no matter how many lawyers he gets himself."

Yeo grinned. "Fawn, are you serious?"

"Yes. According to Ray's research, Michael usually went for those that couldn't defend themselves. I *will* defend them. I *will* make sure he pays. I've let too much go and I'm done."

"Hort has made it clear he will help in any way he can," Cullen said. "Ray's done the research, and we'll keep adding to it."

"He made you sign that pre-nuptial agreement," Yeo reminded her. "You won't get anything from him in the divorce."

"I don't care," she said, voice heavy. "Yeo is his own man and is taking good care of Summer, and Derek has made a success out of his landscaping company. Lowell has a trust fund set up for college from my grandmother. I'll take care of myself. There's nothing of worth to keep me with him anymore. I have a couple of friends in Charleston that will let Lowell and I stay with them."

"No," Summer said, stepping into view of the screen. Her eyes were watering. "I'm so proud of you, Mom. Forget Charleston. Come home. Come to Hobson Hills. You and Lowell can stay with us."

She knelt in front of Ray and grabbed the screen in both hands. Yeo knelt behind her and wrapped his arms around her, tears running down his cheeks.

"Derek could even move his landscaping company here if he wanted. Lowell hates his private school and will like the high school here. You can get a job here."

She sobbed and laughed at the same time. "You could get a job at the Irish Rose. You'd charm everyone's money right out of their pocket."

"Summer," Fawn said tenderly, touching the screen. "My beautiful girl. Do you really want me there? After all I did?" The hope in her eyes broke Ray's heart.

"Yes," Summer said. "I'm Yeo's and Dad's now, but you're still my mom and I love you. I want you here. I *need* you here."

Caden moved to hug her and Yeo. Ray knew the man loved that Summer called him Dad. Gramps sniffled and grabbed his phone, typing furiously. Ray knew he was looking for a house for Fawn and her family. The man couldn't resist.

"Alright," Fawn said softly, eyes full of wonder. "I'll talk to Lowell and Derek this morning. We'll... we'll fly out as soon as we can. Derek may want to stay in Tennessee, but who knows?"

"You may not have to worry as much as you think about money," John said gently. "You heard my wife. She wants Michael Cook destroyed and I'll do my best to make that happen. I'll talk to Cain, but I would be honored to take that bastard down. Free of charge."

"I'll help," Caden said. "You know Cain will too."

"Super lawyers to the rescue," Yeo said teasingly and kissed Caden's chin.

"He'll finally pay, won't he?" Fawn's smile was radiant. "For Dean and all the others he has hurt."

~

A COUPLE OF HOURS LATER, Ray sat next to Dean's bed. His omega was finished with the first surgery and was getting some much needed rest. Marco slipped quietly through the door. "Ray, why don't you go home and get some rest? I can stay with him tonight."

Ray shook his head. "Thanks, but I'm good. Hell, I can't sleep without him next to me."

"Somehow, I knew you would say that." Marco sat and stretched his legs out. "Is there anything I can do for you? I hate feeling useless." He gave Ray a wicked smile. "I really enjoyed scaring the crap out of that Bruce guy that upset Dean last month."

Ray laughed softly. "Bennett and Dean weren't impressed." He shrugged. "I wasn't complaining though."

He heard a quiet jingle and recognized Dean's cell phone. He had forgotten it was in his back pocket. Jackson had given it back to him after calling their friends, Chris and Wendy, in Tennessee to update them on Dean's condition. He reached back and took it out, recognizing Fred Kirby's number.

He frowned. It was four in the morning. "Hello?"

"Ray? I'm sorry to call so early," Min-jun said. "Fred is finally sound asleep. I heard from Wendy that my son was hurt. What happened? Is he going to be alright?"

"Dean is going to recover, Min-jun," Ray said and explained what had happened. "The doctor found out he was pregnant too. Can you believe it? We'll have another baby."

"Is that safe? Wait, I'm sorry. I know he's your omega."

"Min-jun, never apologize for caring about your son. The doctor warned us it will be difficult and it isn't at all safe." Ray's eyes watered as he watched Dean sleep. Marco squeezed his shoulder. "It's Dean's decision," Ray finally said. "He knows I love him no matter what, but he wants to try."

"Dean's decision," Min-jun repeated, voice soft. "You are a good man, Raymond Potts."

"Thank you," he said gently. "When are you going to come see him?"

"I... Fred would never let me," Min-jun said. "He only lets me run errands and go to the church."

"I'm not asking Fred," Ray said. "I can send you a plane ticket or come down and get you myself. You don't have to stay there, Min-jun. If you love Fred and want to be there, then okay, but if you don't, if you want away, we're here for you."

"I want to see Dean so much," Min-jun said. "I'll let you know."

He hung up before Ray could say anything else.

"That was Dean's omega father?" Marco looked curious.

"Yeah," Ray said. "We're trying to convince him to leave his alpha and come stay with us. Dean says Min-jun is like he was and doesn't know he has any other options."

"You let me know what I can do," Marco said. "We'll get through this, alright? Don't be afraid to ask for help if you need it."

The man stood and brushed his lips over Dean's forehead as he slept.

"We love Dean and you," he said, looking at Ray over his shoulder. "You boys are family now."

Ray smiled as he watched Marco leave. The Wilsons were something else. That was for sure.

CHAPTER 13

*D*ean lay back in his bed and stared out the window of his bedroom. He was so glad to be home, but bedrest seriously annoyed him. It was sunny out, and the crape myrtle trees right outside his window were blooming. The lake looked calm and cold, and he wanted to be outside so much.

David Gregor, formerly Bartley, sat at the end of Dean's bed, painting Dean's toenails. All of his family and friends had decided to take turns spending time with him since he had gotten home, whether he liked it or not. He hadn't been alone for a single minute all week. He hadn't been outside either.

David had shown up with his rabbit Cadbury that morning. The rabbit currently hopped around his room, watching Lucy carefully. Dean's cat lay spread out in the window seat with Bonny, tail swaying back and forth. She seemed completely unconcerned with the rabbit. Min, on the other hand, crawled quickly after the poor bunny.

"I'm sorry, cutie," David said. "I know you want outside, but the doctor gave his orders."

"Stupid doctors," Dean said, grumbling.

Okay, so maybe Dr. Little was awesome. The man had managed to fix some of the previous damage to his leg during his last surgery. Dr. Richards was wonderful too, damn it.

David just laughed. "Anyway, I meant to tell you something funny. I was grocery shopping with Harry and Jules a few days ago. We got in line at one of the registers and Jules gets this look of complete disdain on his face. He tugged on my arm and said we needed to switch lines. I was like, what? He looked at the cashier and said, 'That's Linda. She tried to steal Dad's kisses.' Then he looked at Harry and my son said, 'Kisses are meant to be given, not taken.'"

Dean leaned his head back and laughed, not caring that his ribs ached. "I almost feel sorry for her. Oh, our sons are so smart, David."

"They are. Harry really likes Jules." He gave Dean a pointed look. "I mean he *really* likes him."

"I've already had this talk with Jules. They can't get married until they're out of school," Dean said, grinning. David laughed again.

"What's so funny?" Ray came in with a tray full of food.

Dean smelled chicken and dumplings and about swooned. His man took care of him.

"David is trying to marry off our son," Dean said, holding out his good arm and making a grabby hand. "Give me those chicken and dumplings."

"He likes his comfort food," Ray said to David. "Now, none of the boys can get married until they're sixty. They'll live at home until then too. Them's the rules."

"You would break Harry's heart?" David's eyes widened and he fluttered his lashes. He took his own bowl of dumplings from Ray.

"Fine. Harry can live with us too, but he can't take Jules away. I just got him," Ray said. "Oh, what am I saying? Our boys will take over the world. You know Jimmy is looking at colleges, right?" Ray helped Dean sit up, then popped the stands out on the tray, setting it over Dean's lap. "He has his heart set on the Kubert School."

"Sadie is already planning for college too," David said, sighing. "I know we're supposed to be excited and proud of her, but I just want her to stay a kid." He took a bite of his dumplings. "Oh, this is good, Ray." He looked at Dean. "I know your papa is Korean. Do you have any special dishes you want me to try to make you? Comfort foods from when you were a kid?"

Dean swallowed his mouthful of dumplings before answering and forced himself not to push his face into the bowl of yumminess. He was a civilized man, he reminded himself.

"One time when I had a cold, Papa snuck and cooked me kimchi and rice. It was so good. I've only had it that once though. Dad didn't want foreign food in the house. It was Papa's special family recipe."

David patted his leg, then took another bite.

Ray gently climbed into bed beside Dean, making

Beau scoot over in the process. Dean's dog hadn't left his side since he got home from the hospital.

"I fed the beasts this morning, and El Paso got an extra treat," Ray said.

"Don't make my horse fat," Dean said. "Can I go see him today? I'll be good. You can roll me out in the wheelchair."

"The doctor said—" Ray began but was interrupted by Gramps.

"We'll be careful," Gramps said from the doorway, obviously having overheard the conversation. "I'll help roll him."

"Gramps," David said. "What are you doing here? Today is my day to hang with Dean."

"I just finished tilling Dean's garden. Got to take care of those weeds early," Gramps said. "Ray, can we get this boy some sunshine? Please?"

"Please, Ray?" Dean pouted and gave his beta his best puppy dog eyes.

Ray groaned and Dean knew he had won.

"Like I could say no to you," Ray said. "The wheelchair won't work on the gravel, so I'll carry you to the barn. Gramps, can you bring the wheelchair with you? We can set him in it when we get there."

"Wait," David said, jumping up. "His toenails need to dry."

A short time later, Dean was in Ray's arms. He leaned his head against his beta's chest and breathed in the fresh air. Bonny climbed up his chest and nibbled his nose, making him laugh. His guinea pig wore a warm knitted sweater and hat. Beau trotted beside them, tongue hanging from his mouth.

"Thank you, Ray," Dean said. It wasn't comfortable, but damn was it nice to be outside.

"I'd carry you around outside every day if it wouldn't wear you out," Ray said and tried to kiss him. "Damn it, Bonny. That's my man whose nose you're nibbling on."

"You don't hear that every day," David said.

He skipped ahead, carrying Min, and opened the barn door.

"Holy shit," he yelled, jumping back.

Petunia, Daisy, and Dandy ran out the door, oinking loudly. They ran circles around Ray and Dean, making him laugh.

"Did you miss me, piggies? Have the boys been starving you?"

"They sure don't look starved," David said.

Gramps chuckled and set the wheelchair down on the concrete floor. Ray dodged the pigs and set Dean down gently, helping him get settled. He wrapped Dean's blanket around his legs and finally got his kiss. Dean groaned, loving the taste of his beta, and deepened the kiss.

"Do you two need a minute?" Amusement filled David's voice, and Dean smiled as he broke their kiss.

"You have no idea how many minutes we need," Ray said, groaning. "Come on. Let's visit your beasts."

"I think I'll go on and milk the cows," Gramps said, humming a tune. The man loved working as much as Dean did.

"El Paso," Dean said, wishing he could jump out of the chair. His horse hung his head down over the stall door and whinnied hello. Dean stroked his nose, then hugged his head. "You're my good boy, El Paso. You all are." He looked up at Ray and winked. "Especially my Raymondlicious."

"Fuck. Noah was here yesterday," Ray said, hiding his face behind his hands.

"At least I'm not calling you my chocolate stallion," Dean said dryly.

David cackled. "That's his new name. It's decided."

"Why do I like you so much, David? I'm having a hard time remembering right now," Ray said.

Dean started giggling.

"Aww, you know you love me, big guy. Hey, can I take some eggs and milk home with me?" David's heeled boots clicked on the barn floor, and he sashayed down the line of stalls, bouncing Min as he went. He came to a stop, gasping, and spun around. "Oh my god, oh my god. I just remembered. I need to paint your chickens' toenails. I saw someone do it in a YouTube video."

Dean's giggles turned to snorting laughter.

"We can make Jimmy and Jules help him," he gasped. "Oh god. It has to happen, Ray."

Ray sighed. "Do you think Gramps needs help with that milk?"

A FEW DAYS LATER, Dean lay in bed with Summer and

Hannah. Min leaned against him and Beau spread out at the bottom of the bed. They watched cartoons and ate popcorn while the girls cuddled together, wrapped in each other's arms.

Summer shot him a nervous look. "Can I ask you something, Grandpa?"

"Anything, baby girl," he said, smiling gently.

"Have you forgiven your papa for not standing up for you when your dad married you off?" She leaned back against Hannah, eyes full of nerves and confusion.

"Wow," Dean said. "That's a tough question. I guess Yeo told you I've been speaking to my papa."

"Yeah," Summer said. "Mom and Lowell are settled into their house now. Gramps found them one in town. She bought it, but they put it in Yeo's name just in case."

Dean gave her a soft look. He knew why she'd asked her question. "To answer your question, I've mostly forgiven him. I understand why he stayed silent and that helps. I was in that same position for a long time, but I was better at distracting Simon from thinking about the kids." Dean stroked Beau's fuzzy ears and his dog sighed, leaning into him. "I still have some bitterness to work through. I think if Papa did something to change his situation and stood for himself, I would completely forgive him. I don't know if that's fair though. Holding on to anger and resentment doesn't do anyone any good."

"I was so mad at Mom," Summer said. "I thought I would never forgive her."

"You had some good reasons, but it's hard being angry at people we love. They're the easiest to forgive, I think." He thought about his papa. "We want to forgive them. We want to love them and for them to love us."

"It's still hard to see her and be around her," Summer said. "At the same time, I'm so happy that's she's here. How does that make sense?"

"It doesn't have to make sense," Hannah said thoughtfully. "Give it time, and I bet the love will outweigh the hurt."

"I agree," Dean said, nodding. "Your mom made a mistake. She's made a lot of mistakes, sweetheart. Not everyone is strong and brave from the start. Fawn may have come from a wealthy family, but I can tell you, her and I have a lot in common. We were both pushed down as children, forced to squeeze into someone else's idea of how we should behave and think."

Summer took a deep breath and let it out. "She's standing up now. She's being brave and strong."

"That she is," Dean said.

"I'm going to try," Summer said. "I'll give it time, like Hannah said. I'll try."

"Me too, sweetheart," Dean said. "Ask Sadie about Dr. Woodward. It wouldn't hurt to talk to her about what you're feeling."

Summer looked thoughtful. "I'll talk to her tomorrow."

That night, Dean lay back in bed, trying to sleep. Ray's boss had called right before dinner to tell them Michael Cook had alluded arrest. The FBI were flabbergasted. They hadn't thought the man would run. There was a trail leading out of the country, but the Feds didn't seem all that concerned.

Richard had given them all they needed to arrest Vandenburg. Dean didn't know what to think. He wanted Michael to pay for what he had done, but at the same time, it was nice to not have to worry about him.

Ray slept beside him, snoring softly, and Dean smiled, thinking how crazy it was that the sound soothed him. It was like Beau's snores – cute instead of annoying. His dog snuffled in his sleep from the bottom of the bed.

God, he couldn't wait until this damn cast was gone, and he was free to move around, to pet his dog and love on his beta. He growled. He wanted some loving.

He reached over with his good arm and poked Ray. "Ray, wake up. Ray!"

He poked him again.

"Huh," Ray mumbled, waking up. He blinked sleepily and looked over at Dean. "Are you alright, babe? Do you need something?"

"I do," Dean said, pointing at his erection.

Ray smiled wide, then started laughing. "Did you wake me up to give you a blowjob?"

"You said to wake you up if I needed anything," Dean said and stuck his tongue out at him.

"I'll take care of you, baby," Ray said, sitting up.

Dean put his hand behind his head and grinned. Life wasn't perfect, but it was still damn good.

CHAPTER 14

*R*ay slid inside Dean, moaning at the feel of his tight ass squeezing Ray's dick. He smoothed his hand over the gentle swell of Dean's belly. At five months, he was finally starting to noticeably show.

Ray's hand stroked over Dean's chest, and he started to move, slow and steady, in and out of Dean's body. He cupped Dean's face and watched his omega groan in pleasure.

When Dean was finally wiggling and begging in desperation, Ray sped up, angling his hips to slide over Dean's sweet spot.

"Ray!" Dean screamed, coming.

Ray let himself go and pounded into his man. Moments later, he came, shooting hard and filling Dean up.

"I love it when you wake me up, baby," he said, sinking down and kissing Dean.

Dean hummed with pleasure. "Me too." He pulled Ray close and they snuggled up.

Ray spooned Dean and cupped his belly. "What do you think about what Dr. Richards said today?" Their appointment had gone well, but the doctor had prescribed light bed rest. He said Dean could walk, do light chores, and still have sex, but he needed to take frequent naps and get plenty of rest. Dean had stayed silent during the whole discussion.

"I don't like it," Dean said, then sighed. "I've only been back to work for a month."

His leg had required three surgeries total, but it was in better shape now than it had been before the attack.

"I talked to Marco," Dean said.

"Oh, I didn't know you called him," Ray said, surprised.

"He said my job would be there when I wanted it," Dean said. "I offered to take care of some of the paperwork for the ranch here at home, and I think he almost cried. He said I could handle the paperwork as long as it didn't hurt the baby."

"Would paperwork hurt the baby?" Ray smiled, amused.

Marco had been through four pregnancies with Bennett, so the man couldn't be as clueless as he sounded.

"He said mental exhaustion is a thing," Dean said, leaning back and kissing the underside of Ray's chin. "I thought I'd do that until I couldn't. I want the baby to make it, and Dr. Richards said full bedrest is likely to happen in another couple of months. It's so different from my previous pregnancies. I worked hard all the way up to the day I delivered. Then I was back at it the next day. I didn't have a choice."

"You do now," Ray said. "I'll handle the animals in the morning, and the kids already take care of them in the evening. We can even drive out to Ernie's in the mornings and do the morning feeding so you don't miss the damn alpacas and sheep."

"Can we visit with Firefly too?" Dean's voice was so hopeful, and Ray smiled.

Ray had taken Dean to visit him and the others quite a bit while he was injured, and Ray had really liked the horses.

"I, uh, kind of talked to Noah about Firefly. He acclimated to the other horses well and already did a couple of trail rides."

"He still needs me," Dean said stubbornly.

"Which is why Firefly is coming to stay with us," Ray said. "I was going to make it your birthday present, but I can't resist."

Yeah. Jimmy had loved his super early birthday present. Ray had lasted a whole two months before he couldn't resist giving the car to him. The young omega had driven everywhere all summer and had managed not to kill anyone. His driving had even improved.

"Really?" Dean turned over and kissed Ray. "Thank you! I know we have four horses already, but I really love Firefly." He grinned. "Hey, this means you don't have to ride the donkey on our family rides now."

"Excuse me? Jackie is the best donkey in the world and it's my honor to ride him. There will be no other for me," Ray said. "Jules can have his own mount instead of riding Gouda with Jackson. I'm keeping my donkey."

"I love you so much," Dean said as he laughed. After a minute, he calmed. "I'll take it easy, Ray." He lay his head on Ray's chest, voice sleepy. "We'll do what we can until we can't anymore. I'm not even worried. Isn't that crazy? I have you with me, and I know we'll get through this. We'll even enjoy ourselves doing it."

"Hell yeah, we will." They settled against one another and Ray fell back asleep.

The next morning, Ray cooked breakfast for the boys. They were all on summer break, but Jimmy stayed busy with his comics, Jake was working with Marco and Dean, and Jules had become Min's constant companion.

"I'll do all the heavy lifting, Papa," Jake said. "You just pet all of Ernie's animals, okay?"

The boy sat with his shoulders back and a confident grin on his face. *He is just like his papa*, Ray thought with smile.

"I'll drive you," Jimmy said.

"No, thank you," Dean said politely. He leaned over and stroked Jimmy's neon green streaks. "You keep working on my comic book."

Jimmy grinned. "I know you'll like it."

Jimmy and Summer were making a comic book for Dean's birthday. Dean had no idea what it was about, but Jimmy had shown it to Ray. It was about a hero named Cowboy that fought to protect his town against the evil villainess Linda. It was silly and beautiful all at once.

Ray's phone rang and he saw it was Hort, so he answered. "Hey, Hort."

He put the last plate of bacon on the table and made sure the stove was off. He left his family to breakfast and headed to the living room. Betty meowed at him from the mantle over the fireplace, and he saw Pounce's tail swishing from under the couch.

"I wanted to update you all on the Vandenburg case," Hort said. "Richard's testimony, along with all the other evidence, got the FBI their conviction. Last night, Vandenburg was sentenced to life in prison."

"Seriously? I expected a lesser sentence," Ray said. "Not that he deserved one, but he is wealthy and has connections."

"All those connections distanced themselves from him pretty quickly," Hort said. "Good ole Richard got probation and a huge fine. Cook Enterprises is free of Vandenburg, and the board hired their own CEO."

"Any word on Michael?"

"He is out of the country, but the FBI aren't tracking him anymore. He'll get the same verdict as Richard if he shows up. It was part of Richard's deal," Hort said, then laughed. "The Bensons, on the other hand, won't be appeased with probation. They've filed several lawsuits and are also representing three separate individuals that are pressing charges against him for rape and assault. Cook's lawyers are powering up, but the man would have to come back to the country if he wanted to win any of those cases."

"Yeo was right," Ray said, laughing. "Super lawyers to the rescue."

He said goodbye and ended the call, feeling a bit relieved to know the Cooks were reaching their end.

"Dada," Min said from behind him.

He turned around and saw his baby boy had followed him from the kitchen. He carried his stuffed rabbit and his new knitted, purple hippo blanket. Jackson had given it to him at Min's birthday party a couple of months ago. It was Jackson's first foray into the wild world of knitting, and Min never went anywhere without it.

Min toddled toward him and raised his arms. "Dada, up."

Ray picked him up and was rewarded with a wet kiss to his cheek. He carried Min back to the kitchen and enjoyed the view for a minute. Lucy sat in the windowsill, basking in the sun, and Jules curled up against Dean as the two talked about a new outfit Jules and Ernie were making for Bonny.

Jimmy ate while Jake regaled him with stories about helping Dean and Marco fix fencing, and Beau and Lola sat under the table, gobbling up any crumbs that fell.

Tears pricked his eyes as he sat at the table. He had a place here. Each member of his family loved and accepted him. They fit together so damn well. He sat Min in his lap and ate his breakfast, making sure to share little bites with his baby boy.

After feeding the animals in the barn, Ray drove Dean, Jules, and Jake to Ernie's to visit with the alpacas and sheep. Ernie had the summer off, so he had already fed them, but Dean was attached to the brats. They spent some time petting animals and chatting with Ernie before leaving Jules to knit the day away with the other omega.

The next stop was Noah's. Jake was put to work mucking stalls, and Dean went straight to Firefly. He scratched the horse's ears and stroked his nose, cooing at him the whole time.

Ray left him to it and went to visit with Noah. His friend was in another barn, talking with a couple of alphas. He recognized Emmet and scowled.

The damn alpha was Dean's friend. He'd been over to the house a few times and Ray had to remind himself that Dean chose Ray, not an alpha. Emmet was just the kind of alpha Ray had imagined would sweep Dean off his feet.

"Stop scowling at me, Raymondlicious," Emmet said, grinning wide and shaking his head. "I swear you have nothing to worry about from me."

Noah laughed at him. "Have you seen the way Dean looks at you, Ray? I really shouldn't find it so funny to watch you growl at Emmet."

Saul sniffed. "He doesn't even *grr* a little at me. What am I? Chopped liver?"

"You aren't Dean's type, Saul. Sorry," Ray said, shrugging.

"Dad!" Jake came running into the barn, face white and eyes filled with fear. He threw himself into Ray's arms, shaking. "There's a man with a gun talking to

Papa. I hid in the stall, then slipped out. I think he's Yeo's dad."

"Stay here," Ray said, handing him to Noah. "It'll be alright, son."

He ran out the door, Saul and Emmet at his side. None of them had weapons, so they grabbed what they could when they slipped into the barn where Dean was. Ray heard Cook before he saw him.

"It all started with you. Before you, Fawn worshiped me. Then Yeo came along, and nothing has been right sense. You turned my whole family against me, you stupid fucking omega, and I'll make you pay."

"You'll go to prison, Michael," Dean said, calm and steady.

"No," Michael said. "I'm in Morocco, didn't you know? They won't even think of me as a suspect."

Ray looked around the corner and saw them. Michael Cook stood facing Dean. He held a handgun pointed at Ray's omega. Dean stood tall, but Ray saw his shaking hands. Firefly snorted behind him, pounding the ground of his stall with his hoofs.

"Just know, you useless piece of garbage, I'm going to kill all of them, every last one of your spawn. Then, I'm going to kill that bitch of an ex-wife of mine. Your fleet of lawyers can't do a thing to save you," Cook said.

Saul nodded at him, and Ray rushed forward, raising the shovel in his hand and brought it down on the back of Cook's head with every bit of his strength. At the same time, Saul went for the man's gun, and Emmet ran to stand in front of Dean, just in case the gun went off.

There was nothing to worry about though. Saul had the gun in his hand and Cook lay on the ground, empty eyes staring up at them.

"I may have hit him a little too hard," Ray said, wincing.

"Won't hear us complaining," Saul said, voice hard.

They heard sirens in the distance.

"Sounds like Noah called the police," Emmet said.

"Is Jake alright?" Dean started shaking, and Ray dropped the shovel and rushed to pull him into his arms.

"He's with Noah. He came and got us as soon as he could," Ray said and kissed Dean softly. "Fuck, baby, that was close. I should have been here with you. I'm so sorry."

"Don't be stupid, Ray," Dean said. He rubbed his face against Ray's chest. "I didn't freak out. Dr. Woodward thinks the flashbacks happen when I feel trapped. I knew you would come, hero."

"Dean, are you alright?" Tanner and two more police officers walked in, guns drawn.

"We're fine," Ray said. "Saul and Emmet are with us too. The guy on the ground is Michael Cook."

He explained what happened and the men put their guns away.

"Noah is keeping Jake away because of the body," Emmet said, looking at his phone. "He wants his papa."

"Let's get going then. The sheriff will want to talk to you all," Tanner said. He patted Ray on the shoulder. "I'm glad you all were here, and Dean is safe. These guys will secure the scene and gather evidence. I'll give you all a ride to the station."

"Bye, Firefly," Dean said, kissing the horse's head. "You'll get to come home soon."

"He knows about that?" Saul raised a brow and gave Ray a look. "I thought Firefly was for his birthday in September. It's only August."

Ray blushed. "I couldn't keep it secret. I tried, man."

They rode with Tanner to the station, Jake curled up against his papa. Sheriff McKenzie took their statements quickly.

"I've called Gramps," the sheriff said. "I'm sorry, Dean, but me and Gerard have an understanding. If any of his kids or grandkids need help, I call him."

"That means Susan and John will be here soon," Dean said, sighing. "Then the rest of the Wilsons. Why do we have so many friends and family?"

Ray sighed and slung his arm around Jake's shoulder. "I guess we're just so damn lovable."

"Dean?" Gramps burst through the door. "Are you alright, son?" He grabbed Dean and hugged him tightly. "Thank god that man is dead."

"Gerard," the sheriff said, exasperated. "Will you please wait until the investigation is over to say things like that?"

"Oh," Gramps said, leaning back but keeping Dean in his arms. "I meant to say that I'm happy Dean is alright and it's so unfortunate that horrible piece of shit died."

Jake laughed when the sheriff leaned back in his

chair and groaned at the ceiling. "How did you even get here so fast? I called you like five minutes ago."

"Well…" Gramps shifted from foot to foot, then hugged Dean again. "I was already in town, and, um, I have a bit of news."

"Related to the investigation?" The sheriff looked curious.

"No," Gramps said, shaking his head. "I was having lunch at The Cozy Kitchen, but don't tell Zoe that."

"Why not?" The sheriff looked baffled when Ray winced and looked away.

"Zoe is feuding with Gib over pecan pie," Gramps said. "I wanted a bowl of chili, so I snuck in through the back door."

"Pecan pie?" McKenzie arched a brow. "Really?"

"Gib's pecan pie is better than Zoe's," Dean whispered. He covered his mouth, then looked around as if she would pop in from nowhere and yell at him.

"He wouldn't give her the recipe, so she retaliated by serving Yeo's angel biscuits to the morning crowd. They're better than Gib's biscuits," Ray said.

"Now we aren't allowed to eat at the diner," Jake said. "If we do, we face Zoe's wrath."

"You Wilsons give me a headache," McKenzie said, running his hands over his face. "Anyway, what's your news?"

"Well, I was eating my chili and this man walked into the diner. He was clearly out of place and uncomfortable. He had a small suitcase with him and looked scared," Gramps said.

"He needs help?" McKenzie sat up straight, looking concerned.

"Well, he is around my age and looks like an older version of Dean here."

Dean's mouth dropped open and Ray jumped up.

"Min-jun," Ray said. "It's Min-jun, isn't it?"

Gramps grinned. "Yeah. I figured that was him and called him by name. I introduced myself and he knew who I was. Guess you told him all about us, huh? Anyway, I dropped him off at Yeo's to come here."

"Papa came? He really came?" Dean's eyes watered, and he started crying against Gramps.

"Aww, son. Your papa loves you. It took some time to figure out he could be free, but he's here now," Gramps said. "You want to go see him?"

They looked at McKenzie.

"Yeah. You all can go," the sheriff said, eyes soft.

They left, rushing over to The Book Worm. Ray watched Dean and Jake run to a man in his sixties that really did look like an older version of Dean. They hugged and both men started crying.

Yeo grinned and came over. "Gramps said you guys were with the sheriff. Was Papa fighting for your honor again?"

"No," Ray said wincing. "Michael Cook showed up and tried to kill Dean."

"What?" Yeo paled.

"He's dead, Yeo," Ray said. "I'm sorry, but I killed him. He was going to kill Dean, then all the boys, you included. He even planned on killing Fawn. I didn't mean to hit him as hard as I did, but he's dead."

Yeo startled Ray by hugging him. "Thank you for saving Papa, Ray. I don't care if that man was my biological father, you're my dad now, alright?"

Ray hugged him tightly. "I love you and the boys, Yeo. Every last one of you. I'd be honored to be your dad."

"Even if you are only seven years older than me," Yeo said, laughing through his tears. "Papa has good taste."

CHAPTER 15

*W*hen they finally made it home with his papa, Dean showed him around the large bedroom that was part of the new addition.

"We added two bedrooms and another bathroom recently," Dean said. "Ray's best friend, Carter, is a handyman and all our friends and family worked together to get it done in two months. We were going to use one as a guest room in case you came to visit, but here you are."

Dean sniffled and hugged his papa again.

"Jake took over the other new room and we're turning his old one into a new nursery for this little bean." He patted his belly.

Min-jun looked around the room with wide eyes. He carried Betty in his arms. The grey and white tabby hadn't left him since he arrived and purred happily against his chest. Dean knew his papa was feeling overwhelmed.

Min-jun blinked and looked at Dean's belly. "Do you know if it is a boy or girl yet?"

"The doctor knows, but we want to be surprised. Considering I've had five omegas, we kind of expect it to be a little omega. We'll love whatever we have though," Dean said.

"Do you need to sit down? Today must have been horrible," Min-jun said. "I could make you some lunch."

Dean was about to wave his offer away, but he thought about it. His papa wanted to help, to be part of the family. "I would love some kimchi and rice. Do you remember when you made if for me when I was seven?"

Min-jun grinned. "I can't believe you remember that. I'll make you some now. Betty cat, you need to take a nap, okay? I need to cook for my boy."

He set Betty down on the bed, and she moved to the middle, circling around once, then settling down to sleep. Lucy walked into the room and looked around before winding between Min-jun's feet.

"You may be the proud new human to two cats," Ray said from the door.

Lucy jumped up on the bed and settled on one of the pillows.

"Yeah, I think Lucy is yours now too," Dean agreed.

Min-jun covered his mouth and giggled. "I've never had a pet of my own."

"Lucy and Betty are good girls," Ray said. "You'll like them. In any case, we have a surplus of pets around here, so you'll never want for pet love again."

"That's the truth," Dean said and hugged his beta. "Papa is going to make me kimchi and rice."

Ray grinned. "That's great. You were craving it for a while."

"I'll get started," Min-jun said. "Should I make enough for everyone? Do you think the boys will want to try it?"

They walked to the living room and paused. The room was full of people. Susan ran to him and hugged him tightly while he looked around.

Ernie and Jules sat in the window seat, knitting.

"Hey, Grandpapa," Jules said, waving. "I'm knitting you a scarf. It gets colder here than in Tennessee. That's Harry." He pointed to Beau's dog bed. Jules's best friend sat reading a book in Beau's bed. Beau looked disgruntled but lay beside him. "I'm going to marry Harry one day. Papa says we have to wait until we're adults, but Dad said that I have to wait until I'm eighty. It's confusing."

Jimmy and Summer sat around the coffee table, their work-in-progress spread out in front of them. Hannah sat beside her girlfriend, playing with Bonny. The guinea pig was dressed in a purple tutu and chittered away.

"Grandpapa," Jimmy said. "Wait until I show you all my comics. You'll love them. I'm making one for Papa right now and we're adding you to it. It's going to be great."

Jackson nodded from the corner of the living room. They had blocked off some space with baby gates and filled it with blankets, toys, and babies. Jackson and

Olive, Elijah's daughter, sat in the middle, surrounded by toddlers.

Jackson waved at Min-jun and held up Min. Dean's youngest grinned and waved before going back to visiting with his friends – two sets of twins and a Rue.

"We're so happy you're here now, dear," Grammy said. "Ines and I already have your first week planned. We're going to have so much fun."

Dean started laughing, love and hysteria meshing together. Yeo sat in a chair and rocked Nari, and Marco and Bennett were there, but most of their brood were missing. Dean calmed himself.

"Where are all your kids, Bennett? Wait, where's Jake and Linc?"

"Oh, everyone came to check on you, sweetie," Susan said. "Gramps put them to work. Barry, Anna, and most the grandkids are out working in the garden and taking care of the animals. Grey and Ines are poking around the kitchen. I think they're going to cook some lunch. Jake was watching Linc—oh, there they are," she said, pointing out the large window.

Linc ran across the yard, completely naked. He waved his stuffed rabbit in the air and shrieked with joy. Dean could hear his laughter from where he was.

Petunia, Dandy, and Daisy ran with him, oinking and running in circles.

Jake appeared behind them, waving his arms and yelling while Lola kept pace beside him.

Linc just giggled and kept running.

Everyone in the room rolled with laughter, but Yeo just shrugged.

"Being naked is kind of his thing now," Yeo said. He didn't bother getting up. "Jake is thirteen and a mature boy. He can deal with it today. It'll be good practice for him if he ever wants kids."

They watched as Jake stopped and pulled off his shirt, laughing with Linc. Lola started bouncing, and they ran out of view.

Everyone looked at Yeo, laughing.

"Oh, fuck a duck. Jackson, hold Nari while I go wrangle those horrible beasts," Yeo said.

Dean hid his face behind his hands while Yeo headed out the front door. "Papa, I'll show you the kitchen. Grey and Ines would probably love your help, and I want my kimchi and rice."

"Did you say kimchi," Grey said from the doorway. He was eight months pregnant and huge. "I've always wanted to learn to make kimchi. Each person has their own unique way of making it. Oh, Min-jun, please teach me. Please, please, please?"

Min-jun wiped his watering eyes and smiled. "Yes. I need to make some for my son anyway. Come and I'll show you."

He followed Grey into the kitchen, and Dean spun Susan around in circles. "My Papa is home, Susie Q."

They laughed and danced around the room. *I love this woman so much*, he thought to himself. He watched Ray smile and chat with their family and friends.

"Oh, Susan. How can I be so happy when a man died today?" They spun down the hall and into his room.

Susan twirled him around and brought him back to

her arms. "Summer and Yeo don't give a damn about Michael Cook. Can you honestly say you do?"

"No," he said, swaying. "I'm glad he's dead. I know Fawn, Derek, and Lowell were closer to him. Their split from him was more recent."

"I talked to her on the way here," Susan said, pressing his face to her shoulder. "She needs to be alone with Lowell for today, but they aren't mad or even really upset. They're confused about how they feel. It'll be alright with time."

"Poor Derek is all alone in Tennessee," Dean said.

"He has a successful business and plenty of good friends," Susan said.

"He does. I'm going to ask Wendy and Chris to check in with him too. They're good folks." Dean slowed down and came to a stop. "I better sit down and rest a bit."

"You never told me what the doctor said yesterday," Susan said. He told her about the doctor's orders. "That's not horrible, sweetie. I know you dread not being able to do what you want."

"I'll live," he said, shrugging. "I want to do right by my little bean." He patted his stomach. "Dr. Richards said I'll likely be on full bedrest for at least part of the last trimester, so I'll enjoy this while I can."

He yawned. "I need a nap."

"Lay down," Susan ordered.

"Will you stay with me?" He yawned again and pulled the covers back on his side of the bed.

"Of course," she said and climbed in behind him.

She wrapped her arms around him, and he turned around and settled his head on her chest.

"Your boobies are so comfortable," he said.

She laughed and his head bounced. "Go to sleep, Dean."

She stroked his back and he fell asleep.

DEAN WOKE to the best smell in the world. "Kimchi," he said, groggy.

He opened his eyes and sat up. Susan smiled gently, then slipped out of bed. "Do you want me to go get you some lunch?"

"I'm ready to get up," he said. "Thank you for staying, Susan."

"John and Ray came in and took pictures. You were drooling all over my breasts," she said, shaking her head.

"They're good pillows," he said, reaching out and poking her boob.

She swatted him away. "Let's go get you your kimchi."

They left the room and slipped through the full living room. It looked like the work in the garden was done and everyone was ready to eat.

His papa spotted him, and his eyes lit up. Min-jun rushed over and hugged Dean.

"Are you ready for lunch, son?"

"Oh yeah," he said, smiling.

Before he knew it, he was seated in the kitchen,

savoring the deliciousness of his papa's kimchi and rice. Emmet and Saul sat across from him, their own plates full of food.

"I love you, kimchi," he whispered huskily and took a big bite.

"Wow," Ray said from the doorway. "It's come to this. I'm ousted from your heart by a dish of food. I mean, it's good food, but still."

"My heart is big enough for you too, Raymondlicious," Dean said and blew him a kiss.

Ray snorted and kissed his cheek. "I'm getting a plate of that too."

"Sit down, Dad," Jackson said, patting his shoulder. "I'll get you a bowl. You kept Papa safe today."

"He did," Dean said. He looked at Saul and Emmet. "I meant to thank you guys too. Emmet, you jumped in front of me without knowing if the alphahole would get a shot off or not, and Saul, you moved so quickly to grab the gun. Thank you for helping my Raymondlicious save me."

"Anytime, cutie." Emmet grinned. "Stop growling at me, Raymondlicious."

Saul smacked the back of his friend's head. "Ignore him, Ray. Dean, we were happy to do it. You're a great guy, and I'm glad we were in the right place at the right time."

Jackson put a plate full of food in front of Ray. "Dad also located Grandpapa's brother in South Korea."

Dean gasped. "What? Seriously?"

"He had a Facebook account, so it wasn't hard," Ray

said, shrugging. "Min-jun asked me to message him. We'll go from there."

Dean leaned up and kissed his cheek. "You really are my hero."

"You have a good man, son," Min-jun said, refilling Dean's plate. "You have a kind family here. They harvested everything in the garden and tilled it. Then, Grey here said he would use our tomatoes to can us spaghetti sauce. It's his family's recipe." Min-jun hummed and swayed. "It sounds delicious. I've always loved spaghetti. Your father didn't think it was too foreign."

Dean smiled at Grey across the room. "Thank you, Grey. Are you sure that's not too much work?"

The pregnant omega turned away from the sink. "Not at all. I'll make it when I do my own. Easy-peasy."

Jimmy and Drew came into the kitchen from the backyard. A young omega about Drew's age was with them. The omega was utterly magnificent, and Dean recognized them immediately even though they'd never met. Their short blond hair was styled, their eyes were smoky, and they wore shiny pink lip gloss. They wore tight jeans and a beautiful black shirt that was a mix of sheer fabric and lace. Terry.

Jimmy's eyes lit up when he saw Dean.

"Papa," he said and ran to him, hugging him. "Did you have a good nap? I need to remind you to nap, don't I? Ray told everyone what the doctor said while you were asleep. Prepare to be pampered and possibly smothered."

"Do you have any hobbies you can do while sitting?"

Terry asked. "You could knit, read, write, draw, do calligraphy or origami. Oh my god!" He squealed and hopped around. "You could learn Korean so your papa could have someone to share that with. There are a ton of YouTube videos. Where is your phone? I'll start downloading them for you."

Drew groaned and tried to make his friend stand still. Jimmy just laughed and ran to find Dean's phone.

"Dean, this is my friend Terry. They're hanging out with us Wilsons for the week," Drew said.

"Hi, Mr. Dean," Terry said, sitting next to him. "Jimmy is amazing, and I love your piggies. Did you know pigs are the third smartest animal? They don't sweat either, so they have to cool down by wallowing. I like the kiddie pool you have set up in the barn for them to swim in. Jake and Jules introduced them to me. Dandy and Daisy were so shy, but I sat with them for a while, and now they like me."

"That's great," Dean said. "You can come visit them anytime you like. They like to play."

"Thank you," Terry said, grinning wide. "Mr. David and I refreshed the chickens' nail polish too. We wanted to be helpful, and you're supposed to take it easy."

"Terry," Bennett called. He came into the kitchen and spotted the omega. "There you are, sweetie. I see you met Dean." Bennett hugged them and kissed the side of their head. "Jimmy said something about you helping him with YouTube videos."

"Oh yeah, come on, Drew. Let's do this," Terry said

and ran out of the kitchen, dragging Drew behind them.

Bennett watched them go with a tender look on his face, and Dean laughed, leaning into Ray. "When are you adopting them?"

Bennett gave him a guilty look. "Marco and I spoke with Terry's foster parents. They're really nice, so I feel guilty for wanting Terry for myself. I love Terry though. I want to hug them and squeeze them and never let them go."

"Look at it this way," Saul said, taking another bite of his burger and swallowing. "You take Terry, and the foster parents are able to take in another kid. You said they're good people, right? That means a kid in need gets a good foster family."

"Oh, Saul," Bennett said, sighing happily. "I love your reasoning."

Dean ate his kimchi and watched his friends and family come in and out of the kitchen. His papa and Grey bustled around, getting dessert ready.

Beau sat on Dean's feet, and Ray wrapped his arm around Dean's shoulders, pulling him close. Today should have been horrible, but Dean was so damn happy. They would be alright.

CHAPTER 16

*R*ay stood in the bedroom doorway and watched Dean and Jules. Dean was eight and a half months pregnant and had been on complete bedrest for a month now. His omega was utterly miserable.

He was bored, but also in a lot of pain. As his belly grew, the discomfort became unbearable. Ray hated seeing him hurt. That day hadn't been too terrible since Jules and Beau kept him company.

"Read it again, please," Dean whined.

Jules chuckled and held Jimmy's comic book up again. "Alright, Papa."

Dean loved his comic book. Jimmy and Summer had gone all out, putting as much effort into the gift as they did into their own online comic strip and graphic novels.

Ray smiled, then quietly shut the door. He checked on Min. The little boy was taking a nap and lay in the bed with his stuffed rabbit and hippo blanket. Pounce curled up under the crib, taking his own nap.

He went to the kitchen and checked on dinner before making sure Jake and Jimmy finished their homework. It was Jimmy's senior year, and he had decided to take some duel enrollment classes.

"Need any help, Jimmy?"

Jimmy looked up and nodded. "I didn't realize statistics would be this hard. I'd rather take calculus."

Ray sat and started looking through Jimmy's work. He marked areas that were wrong and explained why Jimmy hadn't calculated correctly. He left Jimmy to redo the problems and went back to the kitchen to pull the shepherd's pie out of the oven.

He set it down on the counter, and Min-jun came in the backdoor, flushed from the winter air. He smiled and hummed as he took off his jacket, hat, and scarf.

Ray turned around and crossed his arms, trying to keep the nervousness at bay. "Did you guys find it?"

Min-jun grinned. "Yes. Fawn and Susan helped me haggle with the jeweler too, so we got it for a lot less than expected." He handed the small bag to Ray and danced in place. "Open it, open it."

Ray took the small box out of the bag and opened it. Inside was a lovely gold band. Leaves were carved into it and tiny diamonds dotted here and there like flowers. Nothing stuck out, so it wasn't likely to catch on anything when Dean got back to work. Despite the simple design, it was still beautiful and unique, just like Dean.

"It's perfect, Min-jun. Thank you for hunting it down," Ray said.

Min-jun shrugged and leaned against Ray's side, admiring the ring. "You and Dean have been so kind to me. I'm part of your family now, and you do things for me all the time. Goodness, you're paying for the plane tickets so my little brother and his family can come visit me next summer." His soon-to-be father-in-law hugged him tightly. "I'm happy you let me help you with this. You had to stay home with a grumpy omega."

"We'll have the baby in less than a week," Ray said. "Dr. Richards said it needed to happen sooner rather than later, and the baby is fully developed and in good health. It's scary as hell, but Dean will be happier after he recovers."

Min-jun took his hand and squeezed. "I know you're scared, but Dr. Richards is a wonderful doctor and Dean is a fighter. It will be alright. Now, when are you asking him?"

"After dinner. Fawn and Susan insisted on being here." Ray rolled his eyes. "Of course, Yeo and Jackson want to be here too."

"Grammy and Gramps will be here also," Min-jun said. "In fact, just assume everyone you know will be here and be thankful they're waiting until after dinner."

Ray laughed. "Good point."

Soon enough, it was dinnertime. They all dished their plates and went to Dean and Ray's bedroom as usual. Dinner wasn't dinner without Dean. Ray set up the tray over Dean's legs. His omega's big belly blocked his lap.

"Thanks, babe," Dean said, shifting with a wince.

They ate dinner and chatted for a while.

"I got my letter back from the Kubert School, Papa," Jimmy said.

Ray's eyes widened in surprise. Jimmy had sent his portfolio and application in early, and the phone interview had gone well, but Jimmy had been worried. The stinker hadn't said a word today, just handed Ray the mail like usual.

Dean set his drink down with a thud and shared a hopeful look with Ray. "Tell us what they said."

Jimmy smiled wide. "I got in."

Ray and Jake whooped loudly, and Jules danced around the room with Min-jun. Dean's smile was bright enough to light the room.

"I have enough saved up for tuition and housing for the first year. They have evening classes, so I can still work on the comic strip and graphic novels, which means I can probably get by with minimal loans for the remaining two years. It won't be easy, but I made it in," Jimmy said.

Dean's eyes watered and he held out his arms. "Jimmy, I'm so proud of you. We'll help all that we can, baby boy."

Jimmy got up to hug his papa and Ray smiled to himself. He was so proud of Jimmy saving his money and thinking of the future. Jimmy had put every single penny he didn't spend on gas in a savings account for the past year and a half, and he worked hard every night and weekend on his art.

"Your papa and I have enough put away for your

second year, Jimmy," Ray said. "We've started college funds for Jake and Jules too."

Jimmy's mouth fell open. "Seriously?"

He rushed over and hugged Ray too. Ray tightened his arms around the boy, wishing he could keep him right there forever.

"I don't need to go to college," Jake said, stealing Jimmy's plate while he was distracted. "I'm going to be a cowboy like Papa."

"You have a few years to think about it," Dean said. "We'll see what happens when you're eighteen."

Jake just shrugged and ate his brother's dinner. Ray had a feeling Jake had already made up his mind. Ray could see his son being quite happy with the life Dean and Marco lived.

Movement caught his eye and he looked out the window. Jackson and Yeo waved at him as they jumped up and down. It was time.

"Boys, can I have a minute with your papa?"

They all grinned, knowing the plan, and jumped up. Jimmy grabbed Min from his highchair and patted Ray's shoulder on the way out. Ray got up and sat next to Dean on the bed.

"What's going on?" Dean asked suspiciously.

"We've been friends for a while now and lovers for months. I love you more than anything in the world, Dean. Your kids are my kids, and we have this little guy on the way." He smoothed a hand over Dean's belly.

"Ray? What's going on?"

Ray took the box out of his pocket and opened it. "Will you marry me?"

Dean squeaked and covered his mouth, tears running down his cheeks. "You're asking me to marry you when I'm a big, fat crybaby?"

"You're beautiful, Dean, and I love you. Please marry me?"

Dean sniffled. "I love you so much, Ray, and I'll marry you on one condition."

"Anything," Ray said.

"I want to get married before the baby comes."

"That's in like five days, Dean. I don't know if that's possible," Ray said.

Susan and Fawn pushed into the room.

"It is, it is," Susan said. "We'll handle everything. You'll have to get married right here, but Fawn and I will put it together."

Yeo and Jackson came in next, rushing to their papa's side. "You can get a marriage license in three days. We'll take care of the paperwork for you."

Gramps poked his head in. "I know the county clerk. He'll come here to do the signing since Dean is on bedrest. Can we come in, son?"

"Who all is here?" Dean asked with a smile, waving Gramps in.

"Everyone, baby boy," Min-jun said, going straight to his son's side.

Ray smiled as he watched the man fuss over Dean. The boys piled in next, then Marco and the rest of their friends and family. They stayed a few hours, making plans and celebrating together.

When Dean started yawning, Min-jun shooed everyone from the room, leaving Ray alone with his omega. He helped Dean use the bathroom and shower before dressing for bed.

"I love you, Ray," Dean said, snuggling into his blankets. "We're going to change the boys' last names too, right?"

"Of course," he said, kissing Dean. "Why do you want this all to happen before you have the baby? It's going to be exhausting for you."

"You won't like it," Dean warned.

"Tell me."

"I want to marry you, so don't go doubting me. Now, the surgery should go alright, but you never know," Dean said. "I want you to be the boys' guardian and I've left that in my will. If we're married, it'll make it easier to defend if my dad tries anything."

Min-jun's ex-husband was a pain in the ass. The man fought the divorce and tried to drag it out, but the Bensons shredded him in court. The man had even tried to sue for custody of Jake and Jules. The Bensons had smacked him down, guarding Ray's family as if it were their own, which really, it was. Ray understood Dean's worry.

"You and the baby will be okay, but if this makes you feel better, I understand. I would be honored if the boys took my name. I wish Jackson could," Ray said, settling down beside Dean to sleep.

RAY SAT beside Dean and held his hand during the surgery. Their rings glittered in the lights, and Ray squeezed Dean's hand and took a deep breath, exhaling slowly. He was far more rattled than Dean so far.

"Everything is going well, guys," Dr. Richards said, gaze on Dean's abdomen.

"What do you think the baby will be?" Dean's eyes were focused on Ray.

"I think it will be another little omega," Ray said. "Hell, it could be a little beta or a little girl too."

Ray heard cries. Oh god, oh god, oh god. That was his baby.

"You have a little alpha," Dr. Richards said, amused.

Dean and Ray looked at each other, and Ray started laughing. Tears poured from Dean's eyes as he tried not to laugh or move as they cleaned him and sewed him up.

One of the nurses gave them a look. "What's so funny?"

Ray couldn't stop laughing so Dr. Richards told her. "Dean's former husband was determined to have an alpha. Instead, Dean had four omegas by him. Ray here would have been happy with any gender and he gets the alpha."

"Our poor Jun is going to be the only alpha in the family," Dean said. "Poor baby."

After a while, Ray finally calmed himself. The nurse handed him his son, and he fell in love. Jun was a wrinkled mess with a head full of dark curls. His skin was a warm mocha, lighter than Ray's. His dark eyes were all Dean. He stroked a finger over his son's cheek, amazed at the softness. Min had been just as soft. Damn, he loved babies.

He looked up, eyes on his husband. "He's so beautiful, Dean. We made him. We made this little boy. Jun Josiah Potts."

Later that afternoon, Ray held Min in his lap, cuddling his boy. Min was a little unsure of the baby, so everyone did their best to reassure him.

Yeo stood behind him, hands on Ray's shoulder.

"Mini-boo, we love you and the baby both," Yeo said. "It'll be okay."

Min's lip trembled and he leaned against Ray. He stroked his back. His sweet boy would get used to the baby in time.

Min-jun sat beside Dean's bed with Jackson. Jackson Potts. The young omega had surprised the hell out of Ray and Dean on their wedding day. He had told them he was changing his last name since Ray was his dad now. Ray had cried like a baby.

"Ray," Dean said. "Remember when we met?"

"Yeah, baby," he said, smiling at the memory.

"You made me feel so special. Like I was someone strong. Like I was someone worth caring about," Dean said. "Thank you, for seeing me – the real me."

Ray wiped his eyes and hugged Min before leaning over and sharing a kiss with his husband. "You shine so damn bright, baby. I'm a very lucky man."

OTHER M/M ROMANCE BOOKS BY
C.W. GRAY

The Blue Solace Series – science fiction/fantasy, mpreg

1. The Mercenary's Mate – https://amzn.to/2MAOFEH
2. The General's Mate – https://amzn.to/2G1abRE
3. The Soldier's Mate – https://amzn.to/2S7R6ng
4. The Lieutenant's Mate – https://amzn.to/2THZ47w
5. The Engineer's Mate – https://amzn.to/2HpI4vH
6. The Captain's Mate – https://amzn.to/2knP03W
7. The Rebel's Mate – *Coming Soon*
8. Fire's Mate – *Coming Soon*

The Hobson Hills Omegas – non-shifter, mpreg, omegaverse

1. Falling for the Omega – https://amzn.to/2BgWURV
2. Snow Kisses for My Omega – https://amzn.to/2TdDiol
3. Romancing the Omega – https://amzn.to/2UNENKD
4. Healing the Omega – https://amzn.to/2FNcXrY
5. A Pint for my Omega – https://amzn.to/2XItQf7
6. Unraveling the Omega – https://amzn.to/2xRCnRL
7. The Alpha's Christmas Wish – *Coming December 2019*

Hobson Hills Shorts – short stories from the world of Hobson Hills Omegas

1. The Beta's Love Song – https://amzn.to/2UrRPNN
2. Bennett's Dream – https://amzn.to/2GwSpG3
3. Justin's Journey – https://amzn.to/2DhW1t1
4. Grey's Gift – https://amzn.to/2BcjxXf
5. Hobson Hills Shorts: Volume One – https://amzn.to/2M3oGGZ

The Silver Isles – paranormal, mermen, mpreg

1. The Guppy Prince – *Coming Soon*
2. The Not so Little Merman – *Coming Soon*
3. The Sea Witch – *Coming Soon*

If you would like to keep up with releases, please like and follow me on Instagram (@c.w._gray) or Facebook (@cwgrayauthor), join C.W. Gray's Reading Nook on Facebook, or visit my website at https://cwgray-author.com.